Spinoza closed his eyes, willing the floor to swallow him alive

They were under fire, dammit. Someone out there had the sheer audacity to shoot at him, at all of them. And in the inner sanctum of his empire, yet.

Liguori's words came back to him: "A goddamn sneak attack. Pearl Harbor in the desert."

Spinoza burrowed down, praying for daylight, for salvation, reaching in his mind for some forgotten god, or anything that could transport him far away from there and on to safety.

And from overhead, his answer came: the rolling thunder of a big-game rifle.

MACK BOLAN

The Executioner

DON PENDLETON's EXECUTIONER
MACK BOLAN
The Bone Yard

A GOLD EAGLE BOOK FROM
WORLDWIDE

TORONTO · NEW YORK · LONDON · PARIS
AMSTERDAM · STOCKHOLM · HAMBURG
ATHENS · MILAN · TOKYO · SYDNEY

First edition March 1985

ISBN 0-373-61075-0

Special thanks and acknowledgment to
Mike Newton for his contributions to this work.

Printed in Canada

Only the dead have seen the end of war.
—*Plato*

I haven't seen the end of war. Not yet.
Tomorrow, maybe, or an hour from now,
but at the moment there's a need for action,
right, instead of passive observation. And
the war goes on.
—*Mack Bolan*

Dedicated to those members of a
thirty-five-man special operations force
who were killed by Cuban and Grenadian troops
after making a secret landing in Grenada
prior to the U.S. invasion in October 1983.

PROLOGUE

The action never stops in Vegas. There is always something riding on the line, always the chance to make or break a fortune with another card, another roll of heartless dice across the green felt battlefield.

In Vegas the hunger is never satisfied. With an appetite for money, sex, prestige or power, somewhere in the all-night town a hungry visitor can find it all.

Or lose it all.

Las Vegas is a jungle planted in the middle of a desert, and like any other jungle it is filled with predators. The strong survive by cunning, force and savagery; the weak become their prey, are drained of sustenance and cast aside.

The jungle hunters live within a private hierarchy, self-imposed and rigidly enforced. The strongest and best organized cooperate, divide the lion's share of plunder while the jackals forage for their leavings. Natural attrition thins the ranks and weeds out any predator unworthy of the competition for survival.

Las Vegas is the town that Bugsy Siegel built, and it had been an early stop along Mack Bolan's hellfire trail. He had been tested there and, against the odds, had beat the house. The Executioner had gambled everything in Vegas and he'd won. But his victory was transient, totally devoid of any lasting guarantees.

Now there were rumbles coming out of Vegas, louder than the shock waves from the Atomic Energy Commission's below-ground testing range located north of town. A sinister vibration underlay the omnipresent jangle of the action.

It was time to play again in Vegas, right. Against a loaded deck, with every odd belonging to the opposition. Never mind that Bolan did not know the stakes precisely. There was only one rule in the game he played: you bet the limit every time, and never fold.

It was a death game, sure, and going into it he held a dead man's hand.

With luck and grim audacity, it just might be enough to see him through.

1

Mack Bolan hit a combat crouch in darkness, frozen into immobility among the shadows. His senses probed the desert night, reaching out for any sign of hostile life in the immediate vicinity, found nothing. Still, he did not move for half a minute more, taking no chances.

A cautious soldier never took anything on face value, and Mack Bolan was a very cautious warrior.

Dressed for midnight action, he was virtually invisible among the shadows of the low retaining wall that he had scaled. The blacksuit fit him like a second skin, its snug fabric breathing with him, leaving no excess material to snag on undergrowth or rustle as he moved. His face and hands were blackened with camou cosmetics, leaving only the whites of his eyes to betray him if any foe should get that close.

But none who did would have a chance to sound the warning.

The Executioner was rigged for war. Beneath one arm, the sleek Beretta 93-R nestled in its shoulder harness, specially built to accommodate the silencer of Bolan's own design. Big Thunder, the .44 AutoMag cannon, rode military webbing at his hip, and extra magazines for both weapons ringed his waist in nylon pouches. The pockets of his skinsuit held stilettos and garrotes along with a variety of other tested killing gear.

But the man in black was hoping he would not have to fire a shot this night.

His mission was supposed to be a soft probe, in and

out, staying only long enough to gather some intelligence before he made his exit. In and out, right. Except that soft probes had a way of going hard when it was least expected, turning into firefights in the time it took to draw a breath—or die.

Mack Bolan knew his job. And he was also painfully aware of how "blind chance" could intervene and throw the best-laid plans into the dumpster without warning. So he hoped for soft and traveled hard, a portion of his mind alert for any danger signal on this unfamiliar turf.

The outer wall had offered little opposition, but he knew Minotte would have other lines of personal defense between him and the house. The desert night was perilous, and Bolan was not taking anything for granted so early in the game.

Bobby Minotte was the Dixie Mafia's representative on station in Las Vegas.

Theoretically no one controlled the open city and the different families were free to come and go as long as they refrained from stepping on one another's toes. But Minotte's faction was at least as strong as any of the competition. And he was big enough, for sure, to have a handle on the rumbles Bolan had been picking up for weeks along the covert grapevine. The Executioner knew Minotte could provide the necessary battlefield intelligence if he would talk, and Bolan had unending faith in his own powers of persuasion.

Minotte's private palace in the desert was a rambling ranch-style house surrounded by acres of lawn. The house itself was flanked by stables, where the mobster raised his breeding stock of prize Arabians, and by tennis courts, all dark and deserted now. Despite the hour, the house was still ablaze with lights, and Bolan counted half a dozen cars parked end to end along the curving driveway out front.

The Executioner moved out across the sloping lawn, a gliding shadow, every sense alert for sentries and security devices. He had covered thirty yards, with fifty left to go, before he saw the lookout.

The guy was stretched out on the dewy grass, unmoving, one arm raised above his head, the other draped across his chest. He was either dead or sleeping very soundly.

Bolan knelt beside him feeling for a pulse and quickly ruled out the latter possibility. His fingers found no sign of life; instead they came back slick with blood.

A sharp piano-wire garrote had taken out the sentry. The steel strand was buried in the folds of flesh beneath his chin, so deeply that it might as well have been a knife blade drawn across his jugular. The man had died without a sound, if not without a struggle; his side arm was still snug inside its holster at his waist.

The Executioner felt a tremor race along his spine. Someone else had passed this way within the hour, judging from the body temperature, heading for the ranch house with murder on his mind.

Bolan had no way of knowing who the hunter was, nor his mission, but the final target had to be Minotte. No one with a working brain would brave the *mafioso*'s fortress just to ice a soldier on the lawn and let it go at that.

The capo was the mark, and Bolan was confronted with two equally unpleasant choices. He could forge ahead and take the risk of stumbling into a hit in progress, or he could scrub the mission for tonight and start all over again.

Unpleasant choices, right. But for Mack Bolan there was really no damn choice at all. No question of retreat while there was still a chance of getting what he came for. And if he had to save Minotte's life before he got the chance to question him, fine. It might make the mobster more talkative in the end.

Bolan slid the silenced Beretta from the shoulder rigging, easing off the safety as he moved out, leaving the dead man alone with the universe. Bolan's business here was with the living, and he hoped that he would find some waiting for him in the ranch house.

As if in answer to his thoughts there came a muffled burst of gunfire from inside the house.

Bolan hit a sprint, the sleek 93-R probing ahead of him as he devoured the lawn with loping strides. No time for caution now. If he was going to the party he would have to get there while the host still had some life left in him.

The Executioner was twenty yards out from the ranch-style and gaining when the front doors opened and a man emerged onto the porch. He was dressed in shirt-sleeves, reeling like a drunkard, both arms clasped across his abdomen. His once-white shirt was dyed red from the armpits down, a glistening crimson that was sickly brilliant under the floodlights.

And the guy was struggling to hold his guts in with both hands, no longer able to retain his balance as he sank down on one knee. Someone had done a bit of surgery without the benefit of anesthetic, and the patient was using up the last of his strength in the search for a second opinion.

Incredibly, the man was rising to his feet again, his face an ashen mask from the exertion. Bolan saw him swivel in the direction of the open doors, one hand rising from his ravaged abdomen, a pistol in the fist with bloody streamers trailing from the snubby barrel. The dying man was trying to sight on some elusive target.

Suddenly a slender black-clad figure vaulted through the open double doors, reminding Bolan of a gymnast in midflight. Swathed in midnight black from head to foot, complete with hood and mask, the figure seemed to be armed only with a three-foot-long flashing sword. He came in low, beneath the houseman's trembling gun-hand, bringing the blade up in a glittering arc, almost too fast for Bolan to follow.

One instant the hardman was standing there aiming his weapon at nothing, and then the gun was gone. As was his hand, his forearm, everything, in fact, from his elbow down. It took a heartbeat for the houseman to decipher what had happened, and by the time he recognized the blood pumping from the severed stub it was too late for him to take evasive action. Any action.

The stainless blade was overhead, whistling downward in the time it takes to blink. It made contact with the hardman's forehead, biting through his skull and stopping just short of the shoulders where it met resistance in the jawbone. Satisfied, the swordsman tugged his weapon free and shouldered past the faceless straw man as he took the low-slung porch steps in a single bound.

Mack Bolan spent a frozen moment watching the man's retreat in the direction of the waiting cars. The hood and mask prevented the Executioner from making a secure ID, but he had seen the swordsman's kind before, and Bolan knew a *ninja* when he saw one.

Right.

Now what the hell. . . ?

Before his mind could even formulate the question, three more black-clad figures burst onto the lighted porch. The first two held a struggling form between them, half dragging their reluctant captive over the flagstones. The third, their flanker, hesitated in the open doorway and turned back to face invisible pursuers. From his hip, he raised an Uzi submachine gun and unleashed a ragged burst into the house.

So they were not all armed with swords and strangling

wires, Bolan thought. Their arsenal was broad enough to take in heavy hardware that would make them lethal at substantial range.

The soldier had to decide his course of action, but as he watched the little clutch of moving figures the decision was made for him by pure chance. He caught a glimpse of raven hair spilling around the shoulders of the struggling captive, and the floods provided him a flash of slender leg beneath a skirt as it rode up across the prisoner's thighs.

A woman, dammit. And she was not going with her escorts voluntarily. Whoever she might be—Minotte's wife or daughter, part of the domestic staff—she needed help. And Bolan seemed to be the only game in town.

He pushed Minotte and the mission out of mind, recognizing that a human soul in need was more important than the prospect of interrogating someone who might already be dead inside the house.

Bobby Minotte would have to look out for himself tonight, if he was still alive. The Dixie capo was a secondary target now.

Downrange the submachine gunner was backing across the lighted porch, still firing through the doors and holding back pursuers with his fusillade. Bolan raised the sleek Beretta and stroked the trigger lightly, riding out the recoil, never wincing as the weapon kicked back solidly against his palm.

The parabellum mangler took its target just below the jawline, boring through the mask. The *ninja*'s head snapped back and he was momentarily airborne, making solid impact with the flagstones a second later.

He was dead before he hit the porch and still he never let the Uzi's trigger go. The stubby little autoloader emptied out its magazine in one sustained stream of fire, raking the front of the ranch house and shattering one of the twin floodlights before the hammer fell upon an empty chamber.

The two surviving *ninja* saw their companion fall, but they could not divine the source of Bolan's silent shot. They assumed someone in the house had dropped their comrade so they put on the speed, dragging their hostage toward a waiting Lincoln, whose engine purred softly in the semidarkness.

Bolan swiveled, sighting swiftly. He had a moving target, with the girl still in the line of fire, but there would never be another chance.

The play was now or never—for himself and for the captive.

Bolan took a breath and held it, squeezing the silenced Beretta's trigger. . .once, twice. And he could see the parabellums strike his human target, rippling the fabric of the black costume, boring in to find the man inside.

The *ninja* on the woman's left side stumbled, sprawling facedown on the flagstones, motionless. His partner reacted with the smooth instinctive timing of a true professional. Before the woman could react he secured his grip upon her arm, preventing her from breaking free. With measured strides he kept the woman close beside him, using her as an effective shield until they gained the little flight of steps.

She made her move then, fiercely, desperately, kicking out at her captor's legs, whipping her free hand around to claw at his eyes. She was no match for the *ninja*, but she managed to throw him off balance for a second, gaining purchase on the steps and almost twisting free of his grasp before he had time to react.

The Oriental warrior seemed about to let her go, had actually released her arm with one hand. But before she could break loose, his free hand slashed across and struck her just below the ear with a disabling karate chop. The woman turned to rubber in the *ninja*'s arms, and he half-dragged her in the direction of the Lincoln.

Bolan burst out of cover of the slanting shadows, snarling as he moved. The snarl became a roar, deliberately directed at the *ninja* and his captive now, distracting the attacker before he could gain the car and load her inside.

The Executioner's move was effective, and the slender black-clad figure turned to face him, aware of danger on his flank for the first time. A glance took in the gun that Bolan carried but the *ninja* never hesitated, dumping the woman unceremoniously on the asphalt at his feet as he took up his stance to meet the enemy attack.

One hand dipped down along his waistband, coming up again and flashing forward in a lightning underhand. Bolan saw it coming and went into a flying shoulder roll, rebounding off the new-mown grass and tumbling out of range before the blade sliced air above him.

He came out of the roll with his silenced blaster ahead of him. He milked a searing double-punch out of the autoloader, putting both rounds through the target at a range of fifteen yards. The twin parabellums knocked the man off his feet, one hand raised ineffectually to close the pumping holes above his heart. Another second, and the last reserves of life had melted out of him, his slack form collapsing backward on the pavement.

One left, and Bolan was already veering off to meet the driver of the captured Lincoln when the swordsman reappeared, rolling out of the car and onto his feet in a single fluid motion. Instead of the glistening blade his fist was filled with blue-steel hardware, making target acquisition on the Executioner's chest.

Suddenly the guy exploded, face and chest disintegrating into crimson spray, the useless pistol tumbling from his lifeless fingers. The echo of a shotgun blast from the direction of the porch was painful in Bolan's ear.

He spun around to face the gunner, knowing one man dressed in black would look like any other to the shaken houseman in the heat of battle. Bolan was just in time as the gunner, already working the slide to chamber up another buckshot round, swung his bulky pump gun across to find the second standing target.

The 93-R coughed discreetly and the shotgunner collapsed along the parabellum mangler's flight path, buckling where it pierced his abdomen and tore up his vital organs. He staggered, lost his balance, fell. . . but Bolan did not wait around for confirmation of the kill.

There would be other men inside, perhaps more prowling on the grounds. He had not risked everything, aborted his reconnaissance, to die there in the driveway with the woman sleeping soundly at his feet.

He holstered the Beretta reluctantly, stooping down to catch the woman underneath the armpits. He felt the warmth of a breast against his palm as he wrestled her into the Lincoln through the open driver's door. She was dead weight, and the Executioner needed a moment to get her in position wedged down against the passenger's door and out of the immediate line of fire.

He slid behind the wheel and threw the Lincoln into gear, allowing momentum to close the door behind him as he burned rubber out of there. Before they had traversed the first long loop of driveway, he could pick out human figures in the rearview mirror, milling about the porch and following his progress with their weapons. A straggling burst of gunfire peppered the Lincoln's trunk before he took it out of range.

The driveway straightened out beyond the looping curve and then ran arrow straight across the acreage of manicured lawn. Somewhere ahead would be the gate, which was his only exit now. It might be guarded, but the Executioner was out of options. With the woman at his side there was no hope of a withdrawal on foot.

To the gate then, and whatever hard defenses lay in store there. Running through the darkness without lights, the soldier put his trust in the remaining slim advantage of surprise. . . and in audacity.

Beyond the gate, if he could get that far alive, the desert night was filled with peril and with promises.

2

The wrought-iron barrier was visible at sixty yards despite the darkness. Bolan saw that they were closed, and he could make out moving shadow-shapes to either side. They would be gunners, perhaps alerted now to what had happened at the house. But even if he took them by complete surprise they would still be dangerous.

At thirty yards he flicked the Lincoln's headlights on and kicked them into high beams, pinning the huddled gatemen in the sudden glare. They were collected in a little semicircle, and Bolan got a glimpse of handguns and a sawed-off twelve-gauge leveled at the speeding Continental.

Instinctively he hit the Lincoln's horn and held it down, a warning blaring out against the night, reverberating from the wall ahead of him. It took the gunners by surprise, and they were breaking, faltering, responding with conditioned reflexes that made them move out of the way before the Lincoln plowed them under.

A straggle-fire swept over Bolan's metal steed, most of the rounds going wild or ricocheting off the bodywork. A single bullet drilled the windshield and exploded through a window on the woman's side, but she was safely below the line of fire on the seat beside him.

Bolan held the pedal to the floor and braced himself for impact with the gates. A single sentry failed to get the message or refused to heed it. He was standing at ground zero when the Lincoln's bumper met wrought iron and drove on through, flattening him between the hard unyielding layers of metal like a slice of ham inside a ghastly sandwich.

Bolan had an image of the guy's head poking up above the grille like some human hood ornament, little of him left below the armpits where his body had been riced by impact with the gate. Then he was gone.

The gates buckled, ripping loose from hinges set in concrete. Bolan set his teeth against the grinding, scraping sound as metal tore metal off the Lincoln's roof and sides. Then they were through, briefly losing traction on the gravel of the driveway, fishtailing as they found it again and gained the purchase of the blacktop highway.

They were clear but far from out of danger. Bolan knew he could expect pursuers. He was waiting for them. Still, the speed of their reaction almost took his breath away.

Before the Continental had covered a hundred yards he saw the two pursuit cars in his rearview, one emerging from the ruined gates and then the other, close behind. Their high beams cut a yellow tunnel through the darkness, reaching out and blinding him, until he pushed the mirror up with an impatient gesture.

Both his headlights had been shattered when they hit the double gates. Bolan shut them off, simultaneously killing the Continental's taillights with the hope that pursuit would be a trifle harder. It was dark, with a sliver of moon riding low in the sky. There was just a chance that he could get some mileage out of running dark.

The woman groaned, stirring on the seat, and Bolan glanced across at her. She was coming around, already struggling up through fitful semiconsciousness, instinctively using both hands in an effort to push herself upright. She made a little retching sound, but held her own against the dizziness that gripped her.

Behind them the chase cars were closing, filling both

lanes as they ran two abreast. The wheelmen were pushing it and their passengers had started to unlimber their weapons, trying out the range and scoring scattered hits on the Lincoln. Heavy rounds plunked into the trunk, the fenders, probing for the fuel tank.

Suddenly a Magnum round burst through the broad back window, whistling past Bolan's ear before it took out half the windshield. Pebbled safety glass blew back against his face, the fragments filling up his lap and bouncing off the dash like hailstones.

The woman gave another lurch and sat upright, a perfect target for the gunners who had found their range. Bolan reached across and shoved her roughly down beneath the dash, wincing as he heard her skull make contact with the glove compartment. Still, his companion had the best seat in the house in terms of safety.

Not that it would matter if the gunners on their tail should find the gas tank or hit a tire and send them off the road into a lurching death spin at ninety-plus miles an hour.

Behind the Executioner, the chase cars jostled for position, first one surging forward then the other. Gunners leaned out of both, sniping at the stolen Continental. Some rounds scored, some missed—but they were good enough and close enough to let him know that it was only a matter of time. A bullet clipped the useless rearview mirror off its post and sent it bouncing across the hood; another burned through the seat beside him, grazing his arm before it plowed into the dash.

Bolan hunched his shoulders, trying to minimize the target he presented to his enemies. He braced himself, fists white knuckled on the wheel as he waited for a round to burrow between his shoulder blades.

He played a long shot, easing back a fraction on the gas as he allowed them to close the gap still further. When the closest tail was almost on his bumper, Bolan reached out and flicked on the taillights again, then held his breath.

A long shot, right . . . and it paid off.

The wheelman on his tail mistook the sudden flash of red for brakelights and slammed on his own brakes reflexively, almost standing the Caddy crew wagon on its nose. It drifted hard left, cutting right across the center stripe and jostled hard against the other chase car. A shower of sparks glittered briefly on the asphalt, quickly burning out.

The two vehicles ran along together for a hundred feet or so as the shaken drivers fought to correct. Then they separated, weaving like two wounded dinosaurs, losing precious momentum.

Bolan seized the opportunity and gunned it, pulling away from his enemies before they could recover from their near catastrophe. He used the extra numbers he had gained to put some ground between himself and his pursuers, momentarily losing sight of them as he rounded a curve in the highway.

It was merely a respite, but he had carved himself some breathing room. The enemy would be cautious now, and it could all work in his favor if he played it skillfully enough.

If he was not already leaking gas from bullet ruptures in the fuel tank.

If he did not allow himself the sin of overconfidence that marked a destined loser.

He followed the highway through a series of S-curves, pushing the captured Continental to the limit, feeling her drift on the outer curves as he approached the boundaries of her tolerance. The speed was essential, but he could not risk their lives on unfamiliar highway with a wounded vehicle.

A morning recon had revealed the winding stretch of highway to him. He knew there were five or six more of the looping S-curves dead ahead, but darkness strained perception, played myriad tricks with the mind. Even a conditioned warrior might misjudge, miscalculate, and when it happened. . . .

Bolan dismissed the thought and concentrated on his driving. Two more curves and he would be back on the open straightaway with nowhere in the world to hide or make his stand.

It would have to be soon. He did not intend to let the chase cars tail him back to downtown Vegas. He was not prepared to put his battle on the streets.

Not yet.

The woman stirred again, and Bolan saw that she was awake and watching him. Her eyes were wide with fear, reflecting pinpoints of the dash light as she huddled against the floorboards. There was no time for words of consolation as Bolan saw his chance and acted on an impulse, going for it on his instincts, without preparation or planning.

He stood on the brakes and cranked the wheel hard to starboard as he brought the Lincoln around, rocking to a halt diagonally across the two-lane blacktop. He set the brake and left the engine running, reaching for the woman in the same fluid motion as he sprang his door and shoved it open.

She recoiled briefly, but their eyes met in the semidarkness and something flashed between them. She let Bolan pull her out of there with moments left to spare and followed him on shaky legs as they put the Lincoln behind them in the darkness.

They had barely reached cover—the woman lying prone and Bolan crouching with the AutoMag in hand, when the chase car came into view around the curve. The vehicles were running single file now, but with no loss of speed. If anything, the hunters' anger and frustration seemed to milk some extra RPM out of the straining engines in carbon-copy Cadillacs.

The leader saw his peril much too late, and there was barely time for him to tap his brakes before the stunning impact of collision. Heavy-metal thunder filled the desert night, and Bolan watched an oily ball of flame devour both vehicles along with everyone inside.

The second car was screaming in toward the roaring funeral pyre, but the driver somehow gained control, hit his brakes and leaned on the wheel to put his gunboat in a sidelong skid. The Caddy drifted with its four tires smoking, but the wheelman missed the pileup by a yard or two and came to rest upon the shoulder of the road, his engine stalling.

A single figure staggered from the raging bonfire in the middle of the highway. He was wrapped in flames, a lurching, screaming scarecrow. The Executioner was sighting for a mercy round when a secondary blast rolled out and knocked the figure sprawling, snuffing out the final spark of life.

Doors were springing open on the second Caddy, shaken gunners piling out with weapons in hand but aiming nowhere as they took in the holocaust at center stage. One or two of them were shielding their eyes from the heat, none looking out for Bolan as he drew down on them with the silver AutoMag from less than thirty yards away.

His first round took a shotgun rider in the chest, 240 grains of pitiless extinction ripping through his heart and lungs and blowing him away. His flaccid form rebounded off the fender of the Caddy, touching down beside a startled comrade.

Number two had heard the shot, had long enough to gauge its source and pivot on his heels in that direction before Bolan stroked the hand cannon's trigger once again, dispatching death across the intervening no-man's-land. The gunner's head snapped back and kept on going, portions of it outward bound and lost in darkness. The guy was dead before he knew it, and the Executioner was tracking on to other targets long before the gunner hit the ground.

Three.

Four.

Five.

They toppled like silhouettes in an amusement arcade's shooting gallery, the last one getting off a single shot that never came within a hundred yards of Bolan. The Executioner took a moment to recon the vehicle, making sure that there was no one left alive inside or crouching behind it. Then he slipped Big Thunder back into its military holster.

The probe had gone to hell, and he was nowhere near the battlefield intelligence that he had hoped to gather from Minotte. For a fleeting instant, Bolan wondered if the Dixie capo had survived the hit on his estate. No matter. There would be other sources of information available in Vegas.

The big warrior knew that he would need that information now more than ever. There were wild cards in the game—for all he knew the whole damned deck was wild—and he could not proceed another step along the campaign trail without some hard intel.

The Vegas warning signs were badly out of synch, and he had to get some stretch, some cool perspective to prevent himself from making lethal errors along the way.

One means of gaining that intelligence, perhaps, was already within his grasp. The woman, right. Someone had thought she was important enough to steal her from Minotte and to lose lives in the process. Bolan meant to know what made her worth the trouble.

It was deathly still beneath the velvet midnight sky, except for the hungry crackling of the flames. The warrior made a final fleeting survey of the dead, then turned back toward the living.

3

"I haven't thanked you properly...for everything."

Bolan glanced over at the lady, noting that she had fixed up her hair a little while they drove. She did not look so battle weary now in the reflected dash light and the glaring neon from outside.

"You're welcome," he said simply.

They were driving north along the Strip in Bolan's rental car. Some fifteen minutes earlier they had ditched the captured crew wagon, swapping it for a nondescript sedan, which he had leased for the duration under a cold alias.

"Just like that? You saved my life."

He shrugged it off.

"We both got lucky."

She gave him a quizzical look.

"Well...I guess we ought to introduce ourselves. I'm Lucy Bernstein."

"Blanski. Mike." He paused briefly, considering an angle of attack, then forged ahead by the direct route. "What are you to Minotte?"

She made a sour face and tossed a strand of hair back from her forehead.

"A minor headache," she responded. "I work for the *Beacon*."

"Reporter?"

"Don't look so surprised," she said. "I've been assigned to do an in-depth series on the local Mob, their infiltration into gaming...."

The lady read his face and when she spoke again her tone had gone defensive.

"We're not all in their pockets, if that's what you've heard."

"It never crossed my mind," he told her sincerely. "I'm just surprised Minotte would agree to interviews."

Despite the semidarkness he could see the blush that crept across her cheeks.

"He didn't. Actually, I guess you'd say I broke into his house."

The soldier looked at her with growing interest and a touch of admiration for her courage.

"You don't look much like a burglar."

"It's a last resort," she told him. "But you're right, I didn't pull it off. His houseman bagged me right away. I think they might have killed me...if they'd had the time."

"Minotte had a busy night."

"I'd say." Her voice faltered, the brave exterior slipping out of place. "Mike...I saw him die. One minute he was sitting there and asking questions, then...."

"The hit team?"

Lucy nodded shakily.

"They came in out of nowhere, hacking, shooting... it was like a nightmare."

"Did you recognize them?" Bolan prodded. "Anything at all."

She shook her head.

"There wasn't time. Beyond the fact that they were Oriental...Japanese, I think...."

Her voice trailed off and Bolan heard her fighting to hold back the tears. He felt a tremor at the confirmation of his first impression from the battlefield.

"Go on," he urged her.

Lucy took another moment to collect her thoughts and bring her voice under control.

"There have been rumors lately that the Mob is facing competition from abroad. The Yakuza, for instance. That's—"

"I know what it is," he interrupted, recalling his encounter with the Japanese mobster organization, on a former mission to the land of the rising sun.

She frowned.

"You seem to know a lot. Who *are* you, anyway?"

"Let's just say that I'm an interested observer."

She raised an eyebrow.

"You were doing more than just observing at Minotte's. Not that I'm complaining, mind you."

"Well?"

He felt her watching him as they proceeded for another block or two in silence. When she spoke again her tone was thoughtful, introspective.

"There was an item on the wire from Washington last week...maybe ten days ago...."

The tension spun between them like a taut steel thread as she hesitated before resuming. Bolan felt his stomach turning over as he knew, with sudden certainty, what Lucy Bernstein was about to say.

"It was all about a soldier with a score to settle," she continued. "Seems he doesn't care much for the Honored Society."

"A lot of people feel that way," the Executioner told her, knowing that he could not bluff it out.

"Not many take it this far," she responded evenly. "Fact is, I can only think of one."

His gut was churning, but he kept the tension from his voice as best he could.

"That so?"

She nodded distractedly, seeming lost in her story now.

"I understand that he was out of circulation for a while, presumed dead or some such." She paused briefly for effect, then went ahead. "But now the papers say he's back in action—maybe westbound."

"That's a lot to swallow," Bolan countered, trying to keep it light and flippant, knowing that he missed the mark.

"Up until an hour ago, I thought so too."

He pinned her with a steely glance.

"We were talking about the Yakuza," he said.

She smiled.

"Just rumors, bits and pieces." As she continued, the little smile became conspiratorial. "I might be able to come up with something, given the incentive. Say, for instance, we cooperated—"

Bolan cut her off.

"Where can I drop you?"

She looked stunned as if the Executioner had slapped her face.

"Wait a second, now—"

"Forget it, lady. I'm not planning any media events."

"Well, dammit!"

"Where can I drop you?" he repeated curtly.

Grudgingly, she let him have an address off West Sahara, a mile from the Strip proper.

"Is that home?"

She nodded silently, her profile reminding Bolan of a pouting child.

"Better try an alternate," he told her. "You might have unexpected company."

She got his meaning and the pout softened a shade, giving way to a new rush of fear and uncertainty.

"Oh. I didn't think of that."

Civilians, right.

She shifted in her seat and turned to face him, clearing her throat.

"I've got a friend. She'll let me stay at her place, but I've got to make a call."

He took a side street off the Strip and drove for several blocks until he found an all-night convenience store. He pulled into the lot and waited at the wheel, the engine idling, while she made her call from a phone booth. She was back inside the car within a minute.

"It's set," she told him, rattling off another address.

Bolan put the car in motion, rolling toward the drop. They did not speak at all for the duration of their journey through the desert night.

The warrior's mind was on his mission now—and on the lady, granted. She was civilian excess baggage, and he could not afford to carry her along with him into the hellgrounds. It would spell death for both of them and Bolan was not ready yet to spend his blood without a valid purpose.

Pulling her out of the fire at Minotte's had been one thing—a conditioned reflex. But dragging her back with him into the furnace was a different game entirely. One the Executioner refused to play.

There would be opportunities enough for spilling blood—his own and others'—in the coming hours. Bolan felt it in his gut and in the lifting of the small hairs at the back of his neck as he drove through the darkness, away from the synthetic day produced by glowing neon.

Away from the Strip, Las Vegas lay in darkness, waiting.

There were savages out there, still hunting, most of them still blissfully oblivious to the arrival of their judgment day.

And the Executioner did not plan to keep them waiting long.

4

Bolan sat inside his car with the driver's window down despite an early-morning chill. He was waiting outside a phone booth set against the wall of a deserted service station. The night warrior was restless, smoking in the darkness and checking his watch at frequent intervals, noting the time since he had placed the call to Washington.

Almost ten minutes now, and he disliked the waiting, felt too damned much like a sitting duck despite the knowledge that no one was looking for him.

Yet.

Allowing for three hours' difference in time zones, he knew his party should be up and free to call him back by now.

If Leo Turrin had been able to complete the contact.

If the inside man was able to return his call without attracting any heat or bringing down suspicion on himself.

Mack Bolan cursed the uncertainty and knew that there was nothing he could do about it. Voluntary choice had placed him on the outside, and along with that decision there came certain minor inconveniences, for sure.

And minor inconveniences could get a careless warrior killed.

Bolan sometimes missed his contact with the wily Leo Turrin, once his closest covert ally in an all-out holy war against the Mafia. From his position in the highest councils of the brotherhood, Turrin had been able to provide the soldier with the kind of battlefield intelligence that could be indispensable for someone fighting on the run.

His inside view of Mobland had saved Bolan's life on more than one occasion, and the two of them had grown into a friendship that was deeper than the bond between most relatives.

When Bolan staged his six-day "Second Mile" assault against the Mafia, then disappeared into the Phoenix program, Turrin had been forced to sacrifice his seat at the right hand of *La Commissione*, withdrawing from the Mafia the way he entered it—covertly.

Now Leo Turrin, a.k.a. "The Pussy," was busy riding a desk in the Justice Department. He was a valued asset to the program, with his inside knowledge of the syndicate.

He was riding a desk, right, but Turrin was far from inactive. He had kept the land lines open to Mack Bolan, joining the Phoenix program as an active member. And when the choice came down to bailing out or selling out for Bolan, Turrin maintained their contact on the sly. At need, he could be reached—as "Leonard Justice"—and the Executioner had never doubted Leo's loyalty for a moment. Anything he had or knew was Bolan's for the asking. But the warrior used him sparingly, aware that he could compromise his closest friend and greatest resource, if the Executioner made their fleeting contacts a matter of routine.

And they were back to square one. The war had come full circle for them, with Leo on the inside and Mack Bolan looking in.

Except that there was now a new man in the Mafia reporting back to Justice, leaking out the information that was necessary for concerted moves against the brotherhood.

His name was known to Leo, and through him it came to Bolan.

Hal Brognola's new man on the inside had grudgingly agreed to work with Leo, funneling intelligence to Bolan as the need arose, albeit cautiously. He had a reputation to protect and there were aspects to his underground existence that made Leo's stint within the Mafia look like a cake-walk in comparison.

For openers, the mole—one Nino Tattaglia—was at one time a true-blue mafioso. Whereas Turrin had been trained and groomed for infiltration of the brotherhood and planted in its ranks deliberately by Justice, Nino entered as a true believer, working the underworld for half a lifetime, seeking nothing more than profit and the power that accrued through terror. At thirty-five he had attained the rank of first lieutenant in the Baltimore family of Don Carlos Nazarione before he stumbled into the hands of the Feds on a double murder rap.

The choice Tattaglia received was simple: go to trial and face the death house in an age of multiplying executions, or "turn over," stay inside the family as a mole for Justice.

The choice was simple, right, and Nino went for life without thinking more than twice. If there had been regrets along the way he kept them strictly to himself, and so far, all his information had survived the acid tests devised by Turrin and Hal Brognola.

Bolan had made but sparing use of Nino's talents, tapping in on certain basic information, but declining to involve him in the front-line action, anything that might expose his tenuous position or incline him to think twice about his deal with Justice. Now for the first time the warrior needed hard intelligence about a do-or-die campaign, and he was hoping that Tattaglia was up to it.

They had devised a system similar to the one Bolan used for making contact in his early war against the mob. Bolan would call "Leonard Justice" at a private number, leave some brief message and a call-back number of his own before he severed the connection. "Justice" would connect with Nino on his own through any of several fronts that he maintained for such occasions, and the mafioso would get back to Bolan at his earliest convenience.

Bolan killed his smoke and checked his watch again. There was a chance that Nino would not call. Bolan realized the pressure he was under, living on the razor's edge between the Mafia and the government; an edge honed all the sharper by his off-the-record link through "Leonard Justice" to the Executioner's private war.

As if in answer to his thoughts the telephone began to jangle; shrill tones ripping at the predawn silence of the parking lot. Bolan scrambled from his car and caught it on the third ring.

"Morning, Sticker."

It was the code name he had used with Leo Turrin in the "old days," and it felt good, rolling off his tongue without a second thought.

"Morning, hell," the gruff male voice came back at him. "I'm not awake yet. What's the rumble?"

Bolan smiled.

"Rumor has it that Minotte bought the farm last night."

Surprise was evident in Nino's distant voice.

"Oh, yeah? I hadn't heard that. Who was selling?"

"They're a new firm in town," Bolan told him. "I take it that they're based in Tokyo."

There was a moment of thoughtful silence on the other end before Tattaglia continued.

"Well, uh, maybe I have heard of that, after all."

The Executioner sensed the mafioso's hesitance, realizing the position he was in, but it did not change the immediacy of Bolan's problem, the urgency of his need.

"I need whatever I can get," he prodded.

"Well, there might be something. . .sorta vague, you know, but nothing definite."

Bolan could feel the strain the other man was under, wondering how much to say, what to hold back.

"Anything at all. I'm on short numbers here."

"You've got a guy out there," Tattaglia said at last. "He runs a restaurant or something. Sushi, all that kind of shit. Name's Seiji Kuwahara. What I hear, he's sort of the ambassador from Tokyo. You know?"

"How firm is that?"

"It's carved in stone. Like, maybe, headstones, if he made the move against Minotte."

Bolan frowned to himself. "You hearing war drums?"

"Nothing solid but it's on the edge. Chicago's asking for a sit-down with the Five Families, to protect their investments."

"Is it set?"

"Not yet," Tattaglia responded. "I get the message that somebody in New York is stalling. As to why...."

Nino let it trail away, and Bolan did not pursue it. He had plenty on his mind right there in Vegas, without wasting precious time on the motives of an unnamed "someone" in Manhattan.

"Okay," he said at last. "If you run into anything—"

"Just pass it on to Leonard J. I know."

There was another hesitation on the line and Bolan was about to break connections when Tattaglia spoke again.

"Hey, Striker?"

"Yeah?"

"Good luck. I really mean it."

"Thanks."

The line went dead and Bolan cradled the receiver, staring at it for a moment, mixed emotions welling up inside him.

Instinct told him that Tattaglia was sincere—or getting there, at any rate. And Bolan knew that nothing was impossible. There might be ways to reach the hardest heart, given time and patience.

But right now in Vegas, Bolan did not have the patience to sit back and wait for answers to come calling on him. He would have to hunt them down and find them for himself if he intended to find out what all the rumbles coming out of Vegas really meant.

And if the melee at Minotte's was a preview, open war between the Mafia and the Yakuza could lead to bloody chaos in the streets. He hoped to head it off with swift and surgically precise preemptive strikes.

But in order to accomplish that objective he would need a better handle on the situation in Las Vegas. There were still too many open-ended questions: the vacuum left by Bob Minotte's passing, the role of Seiji Kuwahara and the reticence of "someone in New York" to make a stand.

Mack Bolan had to know the enemy before he moved against him. And for that he needed hard intelligence, the kind that canny warriors use when making battle plans for doomsday.

By the time he reached his car the Executioner was well into a partial resolution of his problem. Bolan knew the source of the information he required. Now all he had to do was go and get it.

It would be simple, just a matter of some skill, some raw audacity, and maybe a helping hand from Lady Luck.

The Executioner was rolling deadly dice in Vegas, and he knew that if he crapped out this early in the game he would be paying with his life.

No matter.

There was only one direction he had always chosen in the hellgrounds. Straight ahead.

The Executioner was rolling on, for all the chips.

5

Las Vegas is a two-faced town. It wears one face by night, another by day. A first-time visitor might pass through the streets at different times and never recognize the city. Looking for the lights, the girls, the glitter, he could lose himself in no time, coming out the other side a different man. . . if he came out at all.

Las Vegas is a different city in daylight. Warm by early morning, temperatures would soar to a hundred in the shade by noon; the streets a wasteland shimmering with desert heat. With dawn all the neon is extinguished and the town takes on a faded washed-out look, more common to a farming town than to a thriving tourist center.

Beyond the downtown Strip the city could be ordinary, even drab—a sprawl of prefab shopping malls and cookie-cutter housing tracts. The scattered slot machines in drug stores, fast-food restaurants and supermarkets stand like remnants of some alien culture, badly out of place and out of time amid the trappings of a workaday reality.

The city lives on gambling but its people dwell apart from the casinos, pursuing separate lives that seldom intersect the fast lane. The rates of homicide and other violent crimes rival cities many times her size, but there are also parks and churches, synagogues and schools. It is a side the tourist seldom sees but warrior Bolan knew the varied faces of Las Vegas.

He knew the gambling mecca was a town made up of

people, sure. The builders and the civilizers. And among them were savages preying on the weak and willing, sometimes turning on each other. But the Executioner stood ready to oppose them on the firing line.

If necessary he would give his life to keep the cannibals confined within their rightful place. And if it did come to that he would be taking many of them with him when he went.

The civic buildings in Las Vegas are as drab as the casinos are flamboyant, and the metro police headquarters is no exception to the rule. It squats on Stewart near the cross-town freeway like a fortress ready to repel invaders—or to keep its secrets safely locked away inside.

Bolan found a space reserved for visitors out front and parked his rental car, the plain sedan fitting naturally with the other cars already in the lot. He spent a moment double-checking his custom fake ID before he locked the Ford and made his way inside.

He was relying on role camouflage to help him through this penetration of what was, in essence, enemy territory. No disguise was readily available beyond the fake credentials, but the soldier knew that with sufficient audacity, and just a dash of luck, he had a chance of getting through it in one piece.

In any case, he had to try.

The human mind interprets everything that passes through the window of the eyes; it color-codes and classifies, provides the connotations that give meaning to the world beyond our noses. Given time, experience, the brain not only "sees," but it begins predicting just exactly what it should be seeing in a given situation, taking certain things for granted in the absence of a jarring visual contradiction.

Thus, role camouflage.

Mack Bolan long ago had learned that it was possible

to manipulate the image that a pair of searching eyes passed on for coding and interpretation. Given static circumstances, the warrior could anticipate what normal minds would "want" to see. With very little alteration in his own appearance, he could readily conform to meet those mental expectations, and the end result, as often as not, was a kind of de facto invisibility that served the Executioner well at need.

And he needed vital information now. There was only one place he could think of where he might obtain it. If it worked he would be well ahead, perhaps securing the handle that he needed. If it failed. . . .

A khaki sergeant on the desk examined his ID perfunctorily and signed him in, providing Bolan with a clip-on plastic tag identifying him as Visitor. The officer steered him through a pair of swinging doors that opened on an antiseptic corridor, and Bolan paced off fifty yards of waxed linoleum until he reached the door marked Homicide.

A nameplate mounted on the office door identified the Homicide CO as Captain Reese. The man behind the desk inside was fiftyish, with thinning hair above a weathered face. He seemed uncomfortable and out of place inside a modish polyester leisure suit. When he stood up the jacket opened, and Bolan saw the Smith & Wesson Model 59 worn on his left hip, butt forward to accommodate a cross-hand draw.

Captain Reese rounded his desk, and Bolan let him eyeball the credentials that identified him as a federal agent.

"Frank LaMancha, Justice."

"Sam Reese." There was immediate suspicion in the homicide detective's eyes and voice. "What can I do you for?"

"I'm with the racketeering task force," Bolan told him, "out of Washington. They sent me out to run a recon, lay some groundwork."

"Ah." His tone was noncommittal.

Bolan glanced around the office, sizing up the man.

"The AG seems to think you've got a problem," Bolan said.

The captain frowned. "We've got our finger on it," he replied.

"Oh? You have fingers on Larry Liguori? Spinoza? Johnny Cats?"

A ruddy color seeped into the captain's cheeks.

"I know the names. We keep an eye on all of them." His frown became a scowl. "You're pointing fingers at a bunch of citizens, and damned important ones at that. Their money talks around this town."

"Who does the listening?" Bolan asked him.

Reese bristled.

"Back off, La Motta."

"That's LaMancha."

"Whatever. I admit we have a problem but we're working on it. What we don't need in Las Vegas is a pack of hungry federales getting in our way with all that 'green felt jungle' bullshit."

Bolan allowed himself a narrow smile.

"I guess you're working on Minotte, too," he said.

"You don't waste any time."

"I can't afford to."

Bolan crossed the room to stand before a wall map bristling with multicolored stickpins. A shiny blood-red pin protruded from the near vicinity of the Minotte stud farm.

"You've got a gang war on your hands," he offered without turning around.

"Says who?"

"Says common sense. You think Minotte's Eastern visitors were wise men following a star?"

"There anything you don't know?"

"Plenty," Bolan told him frankly. "Like where Seiji Kuwahara and the Yakuza fit in."

There was a momentary silence, and when Reese responded his tone was less hostile.

"We're working on it. Kuwahara runs a restaurant on Paradise—the Lotus Garden. We know he's connected, but that's where it ends. No wants or warrants out of Tokyo, nothing."

"What about the hit team?"

"Zip, so far. If we turn anything at all I'm betting on illegals."

"There'll be more where those came from," the Executioner advised him.

"You telling fortunes now?"

"Just playing the percentages. Your town is primed to blow wide open."

"Never happens, fella. No one wants to kill the golden goose."

"The rules are changing, Captain. There's a wild card in the game. No way of telling where the chips are going to fall this time."

Reese stiffened, thrusting his jaw out. "Whichever way they fall, we'll be there."

"Picking up the pieces?"

"Playing by the book, dammit. Chapter and verse."

"So you start out three innings behind."

The captain's face and tone were sour. "Tell me something I don't know already."

Bolan shifted gears.

"I understand the *Daily Beacon*'s working on a series that could turn some heads around your town."

Reese raised an eyebrow. "It's news to me—no pun intended."

Bolan frowned. "You sound surprised."

Reese shook his head. "Not really. Old Jack Goldblume's always got an ax to grind."

"Who's Goldblume?"

"He's the *Beacon*'s owner, editor—you name it.

Likes to call himself the 'Voice of Vegas.' Been around forever. Mostly he takes potshots at the IRS or FBI. He doesn't care much for you federal boys."

"His privilege."

"Yeah." The captain's tone informed him that the feeling might be mutual. "It's funny no one briefed you on him."

Bolan's gut was telling him that it was time to disengage, and he could feel the numbers falling in his head.

"I assume that I can count on your cooperation, Captain?"

Reese's face was devoid of all expression as he answered.

"By the book, LaMancha. You've got your job; I've got mine."

Bolan nodded. "Fair enough. We understand each other."

As he retraced his steps along the corridor to daylight, Bolan thought he understood the homicide detective. Reese had the typical Nevadan's thinly veiled suspicion of the federal government, the world outside the borders of his state.

The local leaders often seemed to see themselves besieged by hostile outside forces, persecuted by the blue-nosed moralists who stubbornly refused to see the silver lining of a legal gambling economy. Reports of mob influence in the industry were commonly dismissed as slander or, providing evidence of guilt was overwhelming, minimized as transient aberrations in a squeaky-clean administration.

Never mind that local politicians from the legislature to the highest of judicial benches had been busted and convicted for accepting bribes from mobsters. Never mind that union leaders closely tied to *La Cosa Nostra* had been climbing into bed with top official spokesmen for a generation now, and federal agents had been lately capturing their antics with videocameras for all to see. Nevadans by and large were still defensive and defiant, stubbornly refusing to believe.

And it was not, Bolan knew, that most of the state's citizens were actively involved in the corruption. Not that they supported it, by any means. But he had seen the same phenomenon in action elsewhere—locals closing ranks against the allegations from outside that seemed to signify a "ganging up" by hostile forces, amounting to a persecution complex in extreme examples.

Bolan hoped that Captain Reese would not turn out to be one of those extreme examples. The captain of homicide could do a lot to help clean out his town if he was willing to admit the dirt existed in the first place. It would take some courage, sure, to go against the men whose money talked in Vegas, but it could be done. With any luck at all, Mack Bolan would be showing Reese the way within the next few hours.

And Las Vegas was all primed and ready for his kind of action, certainly. The different factions of the Mob were at one another's throats and the media was standing by in hopes of giving them some overdue exposure. Everything Bolan needed was in readiness, except a handle on the Yakuza, and what exactly they wanted in this desert town so many thousand miles from home.

Not *what*, precisely; that was obvious in Vegas, the town that skimming built. In actuality the question was more *how* they planned to go about achieving what they sought.

And whether Bolan could move fast enough to stop them short of resolution.

If he could not, then Las Vegas was in for a bloody season of suffering.

If he could—well, there would still be blood enough to go around.

The warrior did not care for the alternatives, but he was used to playing by the rules that others had established for him. It was how you bent the rules that made the game your own.

And Bolan was playing to win in Las Vegas. All the way.

6

Sam Reese slumped down into the vinyl-covered swivel chair and cocked his feet up on a corner of the cluttered desk. His narrowed eyes were focused on the door, but he was seeing Frank LaMancha, hearing him as if the Fed was still in the office.

"You've got a gang war on your hands."

There had been something out of place about LaMancha, something cold and almost deadly in his eyes, his voice.

As if he knew exactly how it felt to drop the hammer, and did not mind the feeling one damned bit.

Sam Reese had pulled the trigger twice in his career with metro, and he knew it took a special kind of man to pop those caps dispassionately.

A killer, for sure.

That was the reading that he got from Frank LaMancha.

The guy was a killer.

The federal agents Reese was used to dealing with were usually clinical, detached, like CPAs examining a ledger full of dry dead figures. They knew their jobs all right, but they were used to working at a distance from the crimes they were investigating, and they generally lacked the look, the *feel*, of troopers long accustomed to the trenches.

But that LaMancha had the bearing of a man who did his fighting one on one. A soldier's bearing. There was a trace of military ramrod in his stance, the posture that a

CPA could never emulate regardless of the guns and badges handed to him back in Washington.

Sam Reese had little love for Feds. Very few had come to be his friends across the years. They were useful in their place—for running operations interstate and such—but they were chiefly skilled at getting underfoot and making simple cases complicated. They assumed an elitist attitude that made them stand aloof from other law-enforcement personnel—and many working cops suspected them of undermining local efforts in pursuit of broader, secret goals.

Sam Reese had put in more than twenty years with metro, rising through the ranks to reach command grade long before its merger with the Clark County Sheriff's Department. He remembered all the federal sound and fury under Kennedy—the wiretaps and surveillance, bugs in offices and counting rooms—all of it leading to a handful of indictments that were bargained down to nothing when they came to trial. When push came to shove the boys from Justice seemed to make their best moves in the headlines, leaking "confidential" information, making allegations, spreading not-so-subtle innuendos.

They must have spent a century of high-priced man-hours chasing leads and fattening their files without approaching a solution to the problem.

And Reese admitted that there *was* a problem. No frigging doubt about it. The syndicate was nothing new in Vegas. Hell, the Siegel-Lansky mob had started everything in '46, and even after Benny bit the big one, there were others standing by to cut themselves a piece of pie.

You did not need a microscope to find the Mob in Vegas—but finding them was one thing; getting rid of them was something else again.

Ironically, the greatest blow against the Vegas Mob

had been delivered not by any law enforcement agency, but by a single dedicated man.

Sam Reese was a lieutenant with Intelligence when it came down and nothing that had happened since had dimmed the graphic memories.

The soldier's name was Mack Bolan, the guy they called the Executioner, and he was famous nationwide for taking on the Mob before he ever came to Vegas. Reese had read about his exploits in the papers, but nothing on paper had prepared him for the grim reality of Bolan's desert blitz.

The captain frowned, remembering the hellfire hours of the soldier's lightning visit, feeling something down inside himself turn over slowly at the memories.

Joe Stanno ran his body shop out of the old Gold Duster in those days. They called him Joe the Monster, and with reason. But he could not measure up to Bolan when the bad shit hit the fan. He called for reinforcements and the Mob sent in the meanest bastards they could muster—no less than the bloody Talifero brothers, with a private army at their backs.

Reese closed his eyes as he recalled the hot reception Bolan gave the brothers at McCarran International. The nervy bastard shot the tires right off their charter jet, leaving twenty guys laid out like slabs of beef along the runway. Joe the Monster lost it all in Bolan's final hours on the Strip, along with half the Talifero team—the other twin got smoked somewhere back East, and the Executioner had left Las Vegas cleaner than he found it.

For a while.

It was not a solution, no. But Reese suspected it was never meant to be.

Acting on his own initiative against the odds, the man they called the Executioner had made a difference in Las Vegas, and that was all that counted.

Part of Reese admired the gutsy bastard, though it

would not do to say so in mixed company. A part of him was almost sorry when the guy flamed out in Central Park.

No, scratch the "almost."

Reese was sorry when the soldier bought it.

Goddamned sorry.

Now the telex out of Justice had arrived, on top of all the other problems he was looking at. It said the Executioner was still alive and kicking ass. No word on where the hell he had been hiding for so long, just a curt advisory to keep the eyes peeled. Bolan might resurface anywhere, at any time, and bagging him was suddenly the number-one priority again.

The Feds thought he was heading west, but then again. . . .

Reese did not want to think about the consequences of a second Bolan visitation. Not with all the crap he was facing on the job. He had a psycho killer on the loose who liked to butcher joggers and another with a taste for little girls. He had a rising murder rate among the Cubans, with a drug war in the offing. Kuwahara's Japanese were squaring off against the Brotherhood—and now he had LaMancha and his goddamned strike force horning in. They would be breathing down his neck at every turn and muddying the waters in their efforts to be "helpful"—if he let them.

"Your town is set to blow wide open."

Great.

He was not losing any sleep about Minotte or his soldiers at the stud farm. Vegas was a better place without them, and the means of their abrupt departure did not faze him in the least.

Old Benny Siegel used to say, "We only kill each other," and for Reese's money, none of last night's crop were likely to be missed. Minotte's "family" would lay him out in style down south, and Kuwahara might be burning incense for his hitters. But to Captain Reese the lot of them were so much garbage, ready to be carted off for landfill somewhere.

He was troubled, though, by what had gone down *after* Bob Minotte and his men were wasted at the hacienda. There was solid evidence of someone crashing through Minotte's gate, but they were *outbound*, and the chase crews all had come to heavy grief a few miles down the highway from the stud farm. No sign there of Kuwahara's samurai, and Reese was wondering if Seiji's action was the only violent game in town.

If not....

There's a wild card in the game. The rules are changing. Shit.

The homicide detective shrugged. No matter, if he had a single mob war brewing, or a double cross—whatever. Reese had no intention of permitting mayhem in the streets of Vegas. It was his damned town, and he would hold the line no matter what.

If they could find a quiet way of killing one another off, the captain would not bust his chops to interfere with family business. Laissez faire was SOP in Vegas, even if the vast majority of locals could not quite pronounce it. Live and let live, even if it came down to dying.

But if the war slopped over from the gutters to endanger innocent civilians, Captain Reese was ready to engage in some constructive carnage of his own. He had a list of names and he was not above some hard harassment, bringing in a few of them across his fender if he had to. Anything to make his point.

It might not come to that, of course. He might get lucky. But experience had taught him that the odds were always with the house, against the bettor in Las Vegas.

Captain Reese knew that there was only one sure thing about the present death game. He had not yet seen the last of brutal jungle warfare in the desert.

7

"I know exactly how you feel."

Frank Spinoza held the telephone receiver away from his ear, trying to mute the caller's strident tones. He rocked back in the leather-covered chair, legs crossed, examining the spit shine on his Gucci loafers and waiting for the caller to wind down a little.

"Certainly I've been in touch," he said when there was a moment of dead air. "The minute that I heard. The families share our mutual concern."

"They'd better," the voice on the other end informed him brusquely. "If the commissioners don't want to fight for what they've got in Vegas, I'll take care of it myself. And there are others who'll stand by me, too, you betcher ass."

Impassive, Spinoza heard him out, even though his gut was churning now, trying out the soothing phrases he had learned by watching, listening as the capos talked among themselves.

But Johnny Catalanotte, as the on-site representative for the Midwestern family, had the strength of an army behind him, and he was no one to fool with.

Unless you had the talent. . . .

"Believe me, John," Spinoza said, turning on the charm, "they're meeting on it now. It's top priority, no question. I'm waiting for their word. . . ."

And he proceeded to lay it on, spinning castles out of smoke for Johnny Cats. He talked an army into existence and had it standing by his shoulder, ready to move when the word was given, assuring his anxious caller that the word was on the way. By the time he finished Johnny Cats, while not eating out of his hand, at least was not gnawing on the fingers, either.

"I'll be waiting, Frank," the man from Cleveland told Spinoza solemnly. "But not too long."

"There should be something later in the morning, Johnny. By the time you get here, anyway."

"I hope so, Frank. For your sake."

"I'm not worried, Johnny."

"Someone better be."

The line went dead and Frank Spinoza cradled the receiver. He found his palm wet where he had been holding the phone and blotted it with clean-pressed linen.

He knew his answers had not satisfied the Cleveland connection. Johnny Cats was still steaming, but at least he was more rational, less primed for an explosion than Larry Liguori, the Chicago mouthpiece.

Liguori was still agitating for a full-scale sit-down to resolve the Kuwahara situation. He would not be satisfied with anything Spinoza said or did until he saw some solid action taken to resolve the problem—preferably by serving up some Japanese heads on silver platters. Now, with Bob Minotte and his soldiers cooling at the county morgue, Liguori's adamant position was immensely stronger than it had been days, or even hours, earlier.

Las Vegas was a powder keg, and Frank Spinoza felt as if he might be sitting on the lid, waiting for it all to blow around him. When it went, he didn't know if he could salvage anything from the debris or not.

If it went, not *when*, he reminded himself. Got to keep thinking positive.

Minotte was on everybody's mind, and Frank Spinoza, though he never liked the man from Baton Rouge, would not have minded something in the way of action, either. But he was under orders from New York to keep the lid on, no matter what. He did not necessarily agree with those instructions—might not even understand them fully—but it was not his place to question *La Commissione*.

He had not advanced to where he was by making waves or making enemies. And Frank Spinoza knew the desert that surrounded Vegas had as many unmarked graves as it did Joshua trees, each one concealing all that remained of someone who had rocked the boat unnecessarily.

Unless he missed his guess they would be planting Seiji Kuwahara and a number of his kamikazes out there sometime soon, and he would gladly read some words above the dear departed...but not before the word came down through channels.

And they would have to be discreet about it. No more Wild West theatrics like last night.

Nervy bastard, that Kuwahara, attacking a man in his own goddamn house at that hour of the morning... coming at him with a frigging *sword*....

A knock on the office door distracted Frank Spinoza from his reverie. He swiveled toward the sound, taking a moment to blot his palms again with the handkerchief, now damp itself.

"Come in."

Paulie Vaccarelli stuck his head in through the door and mumbled, "Sorry for the interruption, boss."

Paulie was Spinoza's "private secretary," in the jargon of the business. He had never heard of shorthand and the only typewriter he was familiar with was usually transported in a violin case. But he was indispensable at coping with the daily problems that arose from managing an empire, and Spinoza valued him.

"What is it, Paulie?"

The gunner frowned.

"You got another call, line two. The Man."

Spinoza felt the old familiar tightening in his stomach but he forced a practiced smile and thanked his Number Two, waiting until Paulie retreated before he reached for the phone.

For an instant all he heard was the bottomless long-distance hum of the line, then the deep familiar voice filled up his ear.

"This line secure?" the caller asked him.

"Yes, sir. Checked out this morning."

Damn the squeak in his voice!

"I've been waiting for some word," The Man informed him, recrimination in his tone.

"I was about to call you," Spinoza lied. "I just got off the phone with Johnny Cats."

A hesitation on the line.

"And how's he bearing up?"

"He'd like to see some action on this thing. They all would."

There was an expectant silence on the other end. Spinoza felt a sudden need to fill the yawning chasm.

"I've arranged a meet for later in the morning here at my place. Just to keep things cool."

"That's good," the caller said, and still his tone had reservations. "It's important that you keep the lid on, Frank. A deal is in the works, but any premature reactions on your end could dump it in the toilet."

"I'm on top of it," Spinoza told him earnestly.

"I hope so, Frank. I'm counting on you. Everybody's counting on you."

The words had their desired effect. Spinoza felt the burden settling down across his shoulders like a physical weight. Unconsciously, it made him squirm.

"Don't worry, sir. I've got a handle on this end, as long as Kuwahara pulls his horns in for the next few days."

The caller's voice turned sharp.

"No matter what, Frank. Keep the lid on. When it's time to move, you'll be the first to know."

"Yes, sir."

"I knew that you could do it."

And the line went dead, the hollow humming in his ear again. As he reached out to cradle the receiver he saw his hand was trembling, and he brought it quickly back into his lap, covering it with his other.

Spinoza sat staring at the silent telephone, skeptical that any deal New York came up with would be satisfactory to all concerned in Vegas. It sure as hell would not satisfy Minotte, cooling in a drawer down at the county morgue. And it would have to be *some* deal to satisfy Minotte's capo now—or any of the others who were up in arms.

Some deal.

Like Seiji Kuwahara's head, for starters.

Frank Spinoza made a conscious effort to calm down. It really did not matter to him what the deal was from New York—just as long as he was on the winning side when it all shook out in the end.

And Spinoza had made a lifelong habit out of choosing winners. It was a knack he picked up on the streets of Brooklyn as a child, growing up wild and mean—incorrigible, they called it—with a father in jail and his mother working at a string of dead-end jobs that kept her out all hours of the day and night.

He did not like to think about the jobs that she had taken, or the price that she had paid to keep him fed and clothed through frigid New York winters. He would have happily repaid her now—if she had not been gone these twenty years.

Brooklyn was a hotbed for aspiring mafiosi in those days. Like now, he thought, but with a difference, right. The old Murder, Incorporated crew was still around the neighborhood back then, still a few good years away from Sing Sing and the chair. It made for opportunities.

Young Frank Spinoza started out by running errands for them, picking up some pocket money in the process.

He had risen through the ranks, surviving several dons along the way and always siding with the heir apparent who appeared most likely to succeed. Thus far his choices had been right on target, leading him to the respected post as New York's top ambassador to Vegas.

Respected, as long as he had the correct answers. As long as he could carry out his orders.

"Keep the lid on, Frank. We're counting on you."

Dammit!

For the first time in his life he had some doubts about his ability to carry out the task he had been given. Doubts concerning whether he could keep the lid on in Las Vegas with so many different pressures threatening to blow it off right in his face.

Spinoza calmed himself, taking a deep breath and looking around his luxurious office, drawing strength from his surroundings. He was equal to the task or he would not be sitting here, about to meet with some of the most fearsome mobsters this side of the Rockies. He could handle them, could handle anything that came his way because he was a born survivor.

Frank Spinoza smiled and felt the tension slowly melting out of him. He was adept at picking winners, and this time would be no exception. If he played his cards right he just might come out looking better than The Man himself.

Frank Spinoza closed his eyes and made a wish.

8

Seiji Kuwahara sat behind his desk, watching the waitress as she laid out the silver teapot and ceramic sake bottle. She lined up the little thimble glasses on the desktop so they were perfectly arranged. He knew that he could not have found an eighth of an inch difference in the spacing of the items before him; everything was ritual perfection, and therefore no more than commonplace.

The waitress finished, bowing her way out of the office. Kuwahara acknowledged her only with his eyes; it would be unseemly and humiliating for him to bow to a woman or an employee. She closed the door behind her, cutting off the normal clatter of the restaurant as suddenly as if a falling blade had severed all the sound waves in midair.

His office had been specially constructed to provide him with a sanctuary in the rear of his establishment, the Lotus Garden. It was soundproofed, insulated—to keep out the riot of aromas that were sickening by day's end—and fortified, in case police or other hostile visitors came calling unexpectedly.

The single door would open only when Seiji pressed the electronic release on his desk. Without it, cutting torches or explosives would be needed to gain entry, costing the intruder any small advantage of surprise they may have had.

And he had had no use for the small fortress up to now, but things were changing in Las Vegas.

The opening guns had spoken. But the first engagement, meant to be decisive, had resulted only in confusion and disappointment. Kuwahara did not think of it as a defeat—although a cadre of his handpicked samurai were stretched out on stainless metal tables in the morgue.

He grimaced at the thought of the cruel indignities that medical examiners, with their shiny instruments, would visit on his soldiers after death in battle.

No matter.

They were gone. The essence of them had departed, leaving only empty shells behind. The round-eyed doctors with their scalpels could not do them any further harm.

He did not grieve for the commandos fallen in his cause. It would have been unmanly on his part, and they were all professionals who knew the risks and took them willingly, accepting death the way a lesser man accepts rush-hour traffic or a minor setback on the job. They had been *ninja*, and they were no more. If he felt anything at all, it was regret that they had died without fulfilling their assignment.

Seiji did not count the mission as a failure—not entirely. The pig, Minotte, lay in the same morgue as Seiji's warriors, and others of that camp had fallen, also. Kuwahara knew that much by way of his informers in the city government.

He knew that the selected target had been badly wounded but Seiji had not meant to lose his first team on the opening mission. It would call attention to him now, before he was prepared to face concerted action on the part of Minotte's surviving associates. At present they were still disorganized—a priceless lone informer in the hostile ranks had told him so—but given time they would inevitably close their ranks against him.

Given time....

Seiji Kuwahara was not afraid because he did not plan to lose the coming war.

He had used the best he had against Minotte, and there were more where they came from in case he needed them. A phone call to Tokyo and he could field a dedicated army, every man a fighter to the death.

But it might be time to try a different angle of attack. Perhaps he should have hired some free-lance Occidentals for the raid against Minotte, he reflected. As it was, the guilty finger pointed straight at him.

He sipped his tea, pushing the problem from his mind.

Now that all the simmering hostilities were laid bare, perhaps he could achieve a final resolution to the conflict. Tokyo was growing more impatient by the day, and so was Kuwahara—though for rather different reasons.

He had learned a lesson from his studies of the Mafia, acquiring insight that enabled him to climb inside the thought processes of his enemies, to see the world through their round eyes and to take their vision one step further.

He had learned the history of the Mafia Brotherhood—an ancient order that found more fertile soil in America. Transplanted from an old and decadent society, the Brotherhood found new vitality there. And with it came an independence that allowed a severing of old roots, the establishment on foreign soil of a distinct and separate empire, larger and stronger than its Old World predecessor. Rich and fat now, decadent itself, the Mafia was ready—all unknowingly—to cede that fertile soil to other, newer growths.

To the Yakuza, for instance.

And to Seiji Kuwahara.

Seiji sometimes saw himself as an explorer, a trailblazer the Americans would call it, clearing out the forest with its tangled undergrowth and making ready for the cultivation of a brand-new crop. So far the clearing process had been sluggish, and he had been working with his hands bound. But he would be free soon, free to use his own initiative and work at speed.

When the crop took root and prospered in the new soil, *he* would be the man on the scene, holding the reins, the power of life and death. He was the pioneer, the pointman, and in time it would be *he* who issued terms to Tokyo.

In time.

But not just yet.

First he had a war to win in Vegas, and the initial skirmish—if not a defeat—was, at best, inconclusive.

He would have to do much better in the future, if he hoped to realize his dream and see it blossom in the desert.

Much better, indeed.

Seiji Kuwahara finished with his tea and reached for the sake. It was time to toast the future—*his* future— and to honor those who were about to die in battle.

BOLAN PUSHED HIS RENTAL CAR along the Strip, northbound toward downtown and the press of Glitter Gulch. The midmorning traffic was already backing up along the boulevard, fully half of the license plates around him representing states outside Nevada.

Tourists, right.

The lifeblood of a state that lived on transients, milking them for every dime they could afford to throw away on gambling, lodging, restaurants and shows.

The pleasureseekers burned up their two-week holidays in search of something—fortune, fame, a chance to be "somebody" for an hour or two.

The warrior wished them well and prayed that none of them would be sucked into the coming cross fire.

Winds of war were rising on the desert, shaping up to blow a hellfire gale in Vegas, right. Between the Mafia and Yakuza, with their traditions of revenge, blood would flow everywhere, enough to drown some blameless souls along the way, for sure, if they did not find the high ground quick enough.

Bolan knew the players vaguely, but he still had only the most general outline of the game in Vegas. It was far more complicated than his former visit to that Monte Carlo in the wasteland. Then, he only had to worry about the hostiles on a single front.

This time he had stepped into a cross fire and he was not convinced that there were only two belligerents involved.

The Executioner knew the formula for an effective penetration strike against the enemy, had had it drilled into his heart and mind by years of grim experience in the field.

Identification.

Isolation.

Annihilation.

The three-step plan that turned the strongest enemy into a vulnerable target. And he was on his way toward nailing down step one.

But the gut was softly telling him that something was amiss in Vegas. He had a general picture of the action from his talks with Captain Reese and Nino Tattaglia. But now, without the necessary detail, he could only thrash out blindly, engaging random targets and perhaps only scratching the surface of the problem.

There was more to what was happening in Vegas than immediately met the eye, Bolan was sure of that much. And perhaps he could narrow it down some more by rattling some cages—seeing how the savages scattered and watching where they take cover under fire.

The methodology had worked for him before—on

other battlefields, in other wars. And he was certain it would pay off for him now.

In any case the soldier meant to try. It was his duty to the Universe.

Warrior Bolan was not fighting this one on his own, had never walked alone along the hellfire trail from the first moment when he chambered up a round and dropped five men outside of Triangle Finance in Pittsfield, Massachusetts, all those many lives ago. The war, which had begun as pure revenge, had quickly metamorphosed into something vastly different, evolving over time, becoming something that controlled the soldier instead of the other way around.

It was a crusade, right. A holy war, in every highest sense of the term.

Mack Bolan fought his enemies and wore his scars because he simply had no choice. He *had to* fight, because he *could*, and in a world afraid to get involved, that made all the goddamned difference.

There was no turning back for Bolan. His war had grown, encompassing cannibals of every stripe, the battlefront expanding to devour the globe. But in his heart, Mack Bolan fought the same fight he had started on the streets of Pittsfield, when he stood beside the family funeral markers and pronounced an oath of vengeance.

He no longer fought for himself, but for all men—the builders and the civilizers who were busy getting on about their lives, too often unaware that it was still a jungle out there.

While the headlines warned them of a danger in the streets, bands of cannibals had organized for systematic plunder and were closing in around them, sometimes in disguise, but always hungry, grasping, never satisfied.

Bolan pledged himself to stand between the cannibals

and their intended victims. He had put his body on the line, a living sacrifice to honor, duty, decency.

The old words, right.

And he had freshened those old words with blood— his own and that of others, spilled in mortal combat, hand to hand.

There would be more to spill before the desert sun went down on Vegas this day. A flash flood, to sweep the wasteland clean—if only momentarily.

The soldier drove with new determination now that the decision had been made. He was taking the offensive, carrying the fire into the enemy encampment, with a vengeance.

And he was starting at the top, damn right.

9

A sullen angry crew was gathered in the meeting room of Frank Spinoza's penthouse at the Gold Rush Hotel–Casino. Spinoza, cautious underneath his best ingratiating smile, rode the headspot at a massive conference table, Paulie Vaccarelli at his right shoulder for support.

The rest were ranged around the table, muttering among themselves. Frank Spinoza could have cut the tension with a meat ax.

On his left sat Johnny Cats, the man from Cleveland, with his able second, Tom Guarini.

Beyond the Midwest delegation Larry Liguori was holding forth for Chicago, pausing now and then to confer with his strong right arm, Mike Teresa.

And opposite the others, set deliberately apart from them on Spinoza's right, was Julio DePalma, sole ranking survivor of Minotte's Southern contingent. His forehead was bandaged with gauze and adhesive tape, giving his oval face a bulky look. He was flanked by two unsmiling hardmen who refused to sit, remaining on their stations at parade rest like a pair of guards outside Buckingham Palace. Julio DePalma clearly was not taking any chances, even in the company of friends.

"I promise you, there will be action taken," Frank Spinoza told the small assemblage.

"Yeah?" Liguori challenged him. "When's that?"

Spinoza spread his hands, a gesture meant to be effusive, which instead made him look helpless.

"As soon as the commission has a chance to meet and talk things over."

Liguori made a disgusted face.

"A chance my ass. My people have been asking for a meet the past six months and all we get is, 'Later, later.' Now it's 'later,' and we got a shooting war, but still no sit-down." He looked around at the others, appealing to them. "I don't know about the rest of you but I'm sick of waiting on New York."

Johnny Cats chimed in at that.

"Damn straight. I don't need anybody two thousand miles away to help me handle Kuwahara and his group. I say we hit the bastards *now*, today, before we wake up dead some morning."

A general murmur of assent ran around the conference table, washing back at Spinoza like an angry surf. He raised his voice to make it heard above the rumble.

"Wait a second. We're not a bunch of punks who run around and just start whacking people left and right. We're organized. We've got a system."

"That's fine," Liguori countered, "if it works."

"It'll work," Spinoza told him sharply, glaring. "Give it time, Larry."

"Time? Give it time, Frank?" Liguori looked incredulous. "Six damn months—"

Guarini interrupted Liguori.

"You're all out of time, Frank."

Spinoza cocked an eyebrow, feigning surprise as he stared down his nose at the Cleveland *consiglière* who had spoken out of turn.

"You speaking for the family now, Tom?"

"He speaks for me," Johnny Cats responded, his voice a rumble from inside his barrel chest.

Spinoza shrugged. "Well, then—you both surprise me. I thought Cleveland had some legs."

"We've got legs," Catalanotte said, bristling. "And

I'm not waiting for some lousy Jap to cut 'em off around the ankles.'' He leaned across the table toward Spinoza, index finger pointed like a pistol barrel. "I won't let anybody sneak up on my blind side like they did with Bobby, rest his soul.''

"A goddamn sneak attack,'' Liguori blurted out. "Pearl Harbor in the frigging desert.''

Spinoza raised his hands again, trying to quiet the uproar with an effort.

"Take it easy, everybody. The commissioners aren't sitting on their hands. No one has anything to worry about.''

Johnny Cats snorted. "Tell that to Bob Minotte, Frank.''

"Minotte was—''

"He was set up, goddammit!''

Julio DePalma had been listening to the hot exchange, and now he could contain himself no longer. Lurching to his feet, he overturned his chair and the two flankers had to step aside as it flew backward, grazing one of them on its way to the carpet. Every eye was on DePalma as he leaned across the conference table, supported on one hand, shaking the other fist at Frank Spinoza.

"Kuwahara's chopsticks set him up and knocked him over while his good friends sat back watching.''

Spinoza fought to control the anger rising in his throat.

"We all know how you feel—''

"You don't know shit, Spinoza. Me, I'm not forgetting Bob Minotte. And my people aren't forgetting, either. We're remembering who iced him, and who let it happen.''

"You need a rest there, Julio,'' Spinoza replied stiffly. "You're talking crazy.''

"Am I, Frank?'' DePalma's voice was balanced on

the thin edge of hysteria. "You think so? Maybe you should think about some short-term life insurance."

Spinoza felt the color flooding his cheeks as he faced the rival mafioso, and The Man's words echoed in his head.

Keep the lid on, Frank. We're counting on you.

He said, "I'll write that off to your condition, Julio."

"Oh, yeah? Well, write this off, you—"

DePalma came for him, had actually begun the move, when something struck the giant plate-glass window on Spinoza's left.

The thick pane shivered, shattered, coming down in a sheet of glistening shards around them, jagged pieces of glass bouncing on the deep-shag carpet, some of them rebounding off the tabletop and causing men to flinch.

But every eye was on the shattered window now, no longer captured by DePalma's rush. Even DePalma himself was staring dumbfounded at the mess, his fists half-raised.

"Well, what the—"

It was Johnny Cats. Spinoza recognized the voice despite its strangled tone and Mr. Cleveland never got the sentence finished.

Because something strange was happening to Julio DePalma. One instant he was standing there, both hands raised as if he had been wakened in the middle of a boxer's nightmare, then he underwent a ghastly transformation right before the gaping eyes of the assemblage.

Julio's face was folding in upon itself, imploding, teeth and lips and nose and all sucked inward as if someone might have pulled the plug and all of him was going down some hideous internal drain. His skull appeared to mushroom outward, bits and pieces of it spinning off in free-flight, spattering the hardmen who still flanked him, staining them with viscous crimson streamers.

DePalma vaulted backward, going through the motions of a sloppy somersault and touching down upon the carpet in a sodden heap. He shuddered once and then was still, no single tremor of vitality remaining in his flaccid form.

Spinoza was still gaping at the carcass on his rug when one of DePalma's hardmen gave a strangled cry and raised both hands to clasp his face. But he was much too late to catch it now as flesh and bone and blood exploded in a pink halo, the compression spinning him around and draping him across the fallen chair once occupied by Julio DePalma.

Only then did Frank Spinoza hear the rifle fire, his conscious mind at last connecting visual and auditory input to complete the picture, danger warnings flashing in his mind with neon-bright intensity. He pushed off from the table, saw the others moving for the cover of the table, of the walls, and on the way down there was just the briefest impression that another body had touched down on the periphery of his vision.

Julio's other hardman, sure, and he was wallowing along the carpet now with red geysers spouting from his severed jugular where steel had triumphed over yielding flesh.

Spinoza felt the carpet on his face, a worm's-eye view with giant furniture surrounding him on every side. He closed his eyes and burrowed down, willing the floor to open up and swallow him alive, to hide him from the rolling thunderclaps and wrenching screams that rang inside his skull.

They were under fire, goddammit. Someone out there had the sheer audacity to fire on him, on all of them. And in the inner sanctum of his empire, yet.

Liguori's words came back to him: "A goddamn sneak attack. Pearl Harbor in the frigging desert."

Spinoza hugged the floor and prayed for daylight, for

salvation, reaching in his mind for some forgotten god or anything that could transport him far away from there and on to safety.

Overhead, his answer was the rolling thunder of a big-game rifle.

TWO BLOCKS DOWN and diagonally across the street from Frank Spinoza's Gold Rush, the Executioner sat back and lifted off the twenty-power sniperscope. Slowly, he let the pent-up breath he had been holding whistle out between his teeth, already reloading the rifle by touch.

The lever-action Marlin .444 held four rounds in the magazine and one in the chamber. It took Mack Bolan something under seven seconds to reload, and he could hear the numbers falling in his mind by the time he had finished, warning him that he was running out of time.

Someone in the hotel below him must have heard the shots. And doubtless, someone downrange at the Gold Rush would have heard them coming in. Along the street below him, somewhere, *any*where, there would be someone on the telephone already, jabbering excitedly to the police, reporting shots, a sniper... whatever.

But the Executioner was not finished.

He had picked off DePalma and his backup gunners, but the soldier was not satisfied with the dimension and the impact of his strike. Spinoza's cage was rattled, right, but not enough.

Not yet.

Bolan had gained access to the roof by slipping on some nondescript coveralls, merging with the listless, faceless maintenance crew that each hotel–casino depended on for life itself. No one had questioned his right to be inside the service stairwell or the overlong bag he carried with him. No one seemed to even notice he existed. He had passed at least a score of paid employees on the way up and not one of them had registered the fact that he was new and out of place, a ringer.

So much for the human powers of observation.

He brought the Marlin's polished walnut stock back to his shoulder, adjusting to the eyepiece of the massive twenty-power, sighting in upon the ruins of Spinoza's penthouse conference room. He could see bodies stretched out and leaking on the rug in there, furniture overturned, the scars of his first wild shot on the wall eight feet above the floor.

It had been necessary to break through the heavy plate-glass window with his first round to avoid deflecting other bullets off the glass. A single 240-grain slug had been enough to do the job, and Bolan had been looking down DePalma's throat before the mafioso knew exactly what was happening.

From there it had been easy.

A simple shot one thousand yards away, beyond the calculated limits of the Marlin's range—but well within the big-game piece's killing distance. Bolan had to calculate the drop on each round that he fired and set his sights above the target, allowing the massive rounds to "fall in" on the human silhouettes with grim precision.

No sweat, sure.

As long as you could work the complicated physics problems in your head while holding your breath and sighting down the barrel of roaring elephant rifle.

No sweat. As long as you remembered that each round you fired was ripping into flesh and bone, separating souls from bodies downrange, sending cannibals to whatever awaited them beyond the pale.

No problem.

Anyone could do it, given years of military training and two tours of field experience as the leader of a hunter-killer team in hostile jungles.

It was a goddamned piece of cake.

He would have thirty seconds, maximum, before someone downstairs could make himself understood on the telephone. Half a minute before the troops started reacting at Metro HQ down on Stewart, only blocks away.

But half a minute could seem like an eternity on the receiving end of Bolan's pinpoint sniper fire.

And they were starting to recover over there, some cautious heads just poking up above the level of the conference table. He started counting once again, marking each of them, verifying faces and positions through the scope. They might as well have been ten feet away from him.

His index finger curled around the Marlin's trigger and Bolan took another breath, releasing half of it, holding onto the rest.

Inside his skull the numbers sounded like a bass drum. But he silenced them with an effort of will.

There was no room for a distraction now. Whatever happened in the next five seconds, Bolan had to concentrate exclusively upon his targets.

He was reaching out to touch someone, damn right, and rattling Spinoza's cage as it had never been before. Anyone who lived through Bolan's shake-up would be looking back across his shoulder from now on, expecting death to strike at any place and time.

A frightened man became a careless man, in Bolan's estimation, and he knew that careless people made mistakes.

In fact, he was counting on it.

Bolan settled into the squeeze, his mind closing the gap between hunter and target before the bullet ever flew. The mental countdown started.

Five.

Four.

Three.

Two.

IT TOOK A MOMENT for the ringing silence to break through Spinoza's mental fog of terror. Lying prone beneath the conference table, clinging to the carpet as if he might somehow fall off the floor, the capo from New York was trembling violently, afraid to open his eyes and face the damage all around him.

But the silence penetrated, finally, and he risked a peek. His first view was a pair of wing-tip shoes, years out of style but still available in certain stores, and favored by a few of his "executive" associates.

He followed them along, over socks and pant legs, rumpled shirt and suit coat, until he found a face.

Or what was left of one.

And he was looking straight at Julio DePalma's.

Somehow the bastard's somersault had brought him back around so that he lay facedown, his head turned to the left as if he had climbed down to check beneath the table for his cringing comrades.

One eye peered back at Spinoza from the scarlet ruin of that never-handsome visage. All else—teeth and lips and nose and everything—had been punched back into a gaping fist-sized hole that no cosmetic job would ever close.

Sealed casket on this baby, Frank Spinoza thought, and he felt his lunch coming up. He turned desperately away from DePalma's leaking carcass, swallowing hard to keep everything inside and taking a deep breath to clear his head.

It almost worked.

Around him others were also taking note of the sudden silence, cautiously rising from their prone positions to assess the damage.

"Holy mother!" He recognized the voice of Johnny Cats. "That nervy bastard!"

There was amazement in the mafioso's voice, but Frank Spinoza was distracted, puzzling out exactly who and what the man from Cleveland meant.

Who was a nervy bastard?

Who had the sheer audacity to raid his penthouse in this fashion, dropping Julio and both his boys that way, scattering the assembled might of the commission's representatives like frightened children?

And the answer hit him like a fist above the heart, bringing lunch and everything back into his tightening throat.

Seiji Kuwahara.

Damn it!

Everyone had seen it coming down to this, except Spinoza.

Everyone except Spinoza and The Man.

Spinoza scowled, wriggling backward from his place of concealment, his mind working a mile a minute now. Suppose The Man *had* seen it coming? Suppose he staked Spinoza out like some kind of goddamned Judas goat, leading the others to the slaughterhouse for some reason that Spinoza could not even fathom at the moment?

No.

It did not track.

There was no reason for betrayal, not when everything was going well for all concerned.

Still. . . .

Tom Guarini was first on his feet, and under urging from his *capo*, he stood up warily, surveying the damage and whistling softly between his teeth.

"You're gonna need a maid up here, Frank," he said, trying for a light tone and missing it by a country mile. "You got one helluva—"

The sentence ended in a plopping sound, as if someone had sliced a watermelon with a cleaver. Frank Spinoza, on his knees and rising, was just quick enough to see Guarini undergo the transformation from a human being to headless scarecrow as his skull exploded into smithereens, wet pieces of it flying off in all directions.

And a moment later Spinoza heard the rifle fire begin again as he dived toward the floor. Inside, he had been half expecting it, knowing Kuwahara would not let them off this easy.

He would make them crawl some more, rub their faces in it, retreating only when he felt the heat.

And where was the goddamned heat, anyway? Someone downstairs must have called police by now. The bastards were taking their time, letting him squirm, sure as hell. Spinoza was certain of it.

The heavy rounds were raining down around him once again and Frank Spinoza ate the carpet, squirming back into the sanctuary of the conference table. He was safe there, for the moment, and he would let the others take care of themselves.

He was planning ahead with the slim edge of rationality he still possessed, thinking past this nightmare and on to the other side of it.

If he survived, there had to be a change of game plan. He had been sitting on the sidelines long enough and waiting for the coach to send him in. Somewhere along the line, the coach had lost his playbook, and the team was getting murdered out there, right before his very eyes.

And Frank Spinoza was not waiting any longer. If he lived—when he got out of this—he would sure as hell be making waves.

A tidal wave that could be felt across the frigging ocean. . . in the streets of Tokyo.

10

It was early evening in the Strip casino, the action heating up as tourists finished dinner or awoke from noonday siestas, coming out in all their finery to try their luck. Bolan merged with them, quickly becoming lost in the crowd.

Fully half the gaming tables were still covered, unmanned—roulette and baccarat, poker and blackjack, the games that would draw high rollers when the tux and evening gown contingent emptied out of headline dinner shows and sought a way to fill the lingering hours of darkness.

For the moment activity centered on the banks of slot machines—the clanking, jangling one-armed bandits that filled up the vast casino with their harsh discordant music. Here and there the flashing lights and buzzers called attention to a jackpot winner, bringing momentary interruption to the action as the other players paused to look in the direction of the lights and Klaxons, paying homage briefly or else cursing underneath their breaths, then turning back with new determination to their own machines.

The neon sign out front lured devotees to try the "Liberal Slots" by promising a "ninety-seven percent return" on house machines. No small print there to clarify the message but the locals understood it well enough. The slots were never meant to pay off ninety-seven percent of the time—and never did; rather, ninety-seven percent of the slots could be expected to pay off in some amount, sometime. As for the other three percent. . . .

House odds, damn right.

It was the name of the game.

Bolan crossed the casino floor, rubbing shoulders with the players and security guards—some of them county deputies moonlighting in the private sector. He followed lighted signs to the Tahitian Lounge and found the double doors already closed, the dinner show in progress. Brushing past a life-sized cutout of the grinning star, a stand-up comic billed as "The Ethnologist," he slipped inside the semidarkness of the showroom. Through the murk, a maître d' in full black-tie regalia moved to intercept him.

"I'm sorry, sir—"

The soldier palmed a fifty, made the handoff smoothly.

"Don't be. And never mind the table. I'm just passing through."

All smiles now, pocketing the cash.

"Of course, sir, as you say."

The showroom was a horseshoe layout with the rows of mess-hall tables ranged along declining tiers, the stage some fifty yards downrange at center field. Bolan moved to his left, keeping to a narrow aisle that ran along the wall, moving on until he reached the curtained door that led backstage.

The wings were crowded, bustling with musicians, stagehands, nearly naked dancers and a juggler sorting through a crate of sharp-edged kitchen instruments. A pair of six-foot-tall show girls wearing spangled capes and very little else were standing in the wings, and Bolan found a place behind them in the shadows, concentrating on the lone performer occupying center stage.

"Now, I'm not no ethnician, but. . . ."

A ripple of anticipatory laughter fanned out through the audience and Tommy Anders waited for it to swell, then subside, before he continued with his routine. It was the comic's trade line, and it never failed to preface a lampoon against the dark, ironic side of the American melting pot.

Anders had been successful for a score of years with his routines that gaffed the sacred cows of ethnic sensitivity. His talent for expounding on the obvious made him a six-figure draw in Miami, Las Vegas, Atlantic City.

He was also on another, secret payroll circulated out of Washington, D.C. And as an agent of the Justice Department's Sensitive Operations Group, he had participated in a number of the Executioner's campaigns against the Mafia.

And it had all begun some years before in Vegas.

"I'm not no ethnician," he was saying, "but have you noticed how the Japanese are taking over everything these days? I mean it. Thumbing through a catalog at Monkey Wards, you might as well be looking at the Yellow Pages in a phone booth down at Tokyo and Vine."

Another pause for the laughter, rising now as the audience warmed to his subject.

"Just look at all the patriotic brand names that we're dealing with today." And he was counting on the fingers of one hand as he continued. "There's Akai, Datsun, Honda, Isuzu and Kawasaki, Nikon and Sanyo, Sony and Subaru, Toyota and Yashica."

By the time he finished the roster everyone in the audience was laughing, drowning out the ice-cube rattle from their cocktails.

"They've even got a Hirohito doll due out for Christmas now, I mean it," Anders continued. "Would I lie to you? You wind him up, he takes some snapshots of your town—and then he buys it."

He paused onstage, waiting for the uproar to die down. There was some appreciative applause amid the laughter now.

"I'll tell you honestly, it's getting so a real American just can't keep up with competition from the East. They tell me that the Japanese are even competing with the Mafia these days. I mean it. Honestly, now, I'm not anti-ethnic, but—" the other trade line and the audience responded on cue "—we've got to draw the line somewhere and it might as well be in the gutter, right? I mean, who needs a godfather who can't pronounce lasagna?"

He had them and the comic had no intention of letting his audience go until the point was made.

"You ever try to toss a body from a speeding rickshaw? Jeez, it's murder on the coolies. Seriously, though, I understand the Mob is getting nervous nowadays. Some of them are mixing sake in with their spaghetti sauce...."

The music and laughter came up together, and Tommy Anders began to disengage himself from the crowd, thanking them for their attention and waving toward the rear.

Around him the spotlights had begun to dance, and Bolan's show girls moved out onto the stage, distracting the faithful while a similar contingent emerged from the wings on the other side. He broke off an appreciative parting glance and made his way back toward the dressing rooms.

He did not miss the three torpedoes lounging near the door with Tommy Anders's name displayed in cardboard glitter. They were slickly dressed, neatly groomed, hard of eye—and they were Japanese.

Mack Bolan casually moved on past them, feeling eyes on his back studying him, sizing him up and filing him away for future reference. He found a corner farther down and ambled on around it.

Tommy Anders would be close behind him now, and Bolan could afford to wait, observing what transpired when East met West.

Another five long minutes passed before the ethnologist arrived, and there was caution in his stride as he ap-

proached the Japanese contingent, concern disguised
beneath the usual glad-hand smile. He made some off-
hand comment to the delegates from Tokyo—Bolan
could not catch the words—and then the trio formed a
semicircle blocking his admission to the dressing room.

The tallest of them took the middle, reaching out and
jabbing Anders in the chest with one slim finger, punc-
tuating whatever it was he was saying to the comic.

And Tommy Anders was no longer smiling.

Bolan reemerged from cover, closing quietly and
keeping to the blind side of his adversaries. Anders saw
him coming and relief was visible on his face beneath
the show of mounting irritation.

When he was half a dozen paces out and ready, Bolan
made his presence known to all concerned.

"What's this?" he asked. "Somebody order take-
out?"

The three torpedoes spun to face him, all off guard
but recovering swiftly, professionally. The leader came
at Bolan without preamble, launching himself at the
Executioner's face in a flying kick that transformed his
body into a hurtling projectile.

The jungle fighter sidestepped, going underneath the
lethal legs and bringing up an elbow in the process, digging hard and deep against the other's kidneys as he
hurtled past.

The guy lost balance, wobbled in midair and touched
down hard upon the concrete floor, his silk suit offering
no traction. He slid into collision with some standing
scenery, which collapsed around him. His partners
watched for half a heartbeat, sizing up the situation,
then they made their move.

One of them made straight for Bolan and the other
turned on Anders, bringing both hands up in the tradi-
tional karate stance. There was no time for Bolan to
check out the comic's response now, not while he was

fighting for his life against a pro who obviously knew the moves.

But there is still a difference, right, between rehearsing in a gym and working out on humans who have nothing left to lose except their lives. A punching bag will never sidestep, never slam a rabbit-punch into your kidneys when you least expect it—and the training only takes you so far toward the razor's edge of combat.

Bolan on the other hand had been there many times, and he had always come back from the edge victorious. Sometimes he was severely wounded, but the Executioner knew that injury in battle could make a tougher, stronger soldier in the end.

He had picked up the moves from experts in the Orient and then refined them on his own through years of combat trial and error. And if the Executioner was no Bruce Lee, his adversary was no goddamned Mack Bolan, either.

Bolan saw the hard hand flashing toward his face and feinted left, going in below it, driving bone and sinew into yielding ribs with all his might. The thin opponent doubled over, retching, gasping for a breath, but the Man from Blood was not through with him yet.

No way.

Bolan seized a wrist—the one that had been meant to drive bare knuckles through his face—and twisted, bringing the arm out to full stiff extension. He wrenched it up and back until the socket yielded, and at the same instant drove his full weight down onto the elbow in a power smash.

There was a matchstick cracking sound, a strangled scream, and pain drove Bolan's adversary to his knees. The useless arm hung slack against his side, its outline now reminding Bolan of a cartoon figure's arm, just caught inside a door.

The guy was sobbing, and the Executioner put him

under with a swift kick to the head, his heel impacting on the temple of that would-be samurai and driving him against the nearest wall where he lay slack and flaccid like a leaky bag of grain.

When Bolan looked, the comic already had his man on the ropes, employing moves they never taught in any comedy school. A slashing right cross dropped the hoodlum in his tracks, and Anders stepped over his prostrate form to survey the field, looking for other contestants.

"Want to leave them here?" the comic asked. "We've got a good custodian."

"Why not," the Man from Blood responded. "Use a drink?"

"I thought you'd never ask. Just let me change."

Bolan followed Tommy Anders through the narrow door into his dressing room. Behind them, three of Tokyo's finest were stretched out on the cold cement, already drawing curious show girls and stagehands. As the door closed behind him, Bolan heard them calling for someone to fetch security, an ambulance.

The numbers, right.

He heard them running now, and he was running out of time in Vegas.

This had been a skirmish, but it would be suicidal to hang around and answer questions for police.

Tommy Anders recognized the urgency and kept his quick-change to a minimum, having Bolan in and out of there in something less than one minute flat. They were well along their way in the direction of the parking lot before security arrived to deal with their attackers.

Outside, the desert night was cooling off despite the blood-red fire of glaring neon. By midnight, you could freeze to death beyond the city.

But for Vegas this night, Bolan forecast heat enough to burn some houses down. Enough perhaps, to warm the whole damned town.

11

"We've played this scene before, you know."

Mack Bolan smiled and sipped his coffee, making one more scan of the perimeter around the all-night drive-in restaurant.

"I thought it looked familiar."

And the Executioner could not escape a certain sense of déjà vu, right, sitting there with Anders in the rental Ford. A sense that he had seen and done it all, been through it all before with the comic.

Their initial meeting had been backstage from a Vegas showroom, all those lives ago, and Anders had been feeling pressure that time, too. The heat was coming from a pair of Mafia sluggers then, and Bolan had pulled him out from under. They had cooperated on that first campaign in Vegas, and later when they met again in Honolulu, Anders had rendered valuable aid to Bolan's hellfire effort on another front.

He was an ally, right, and so much more.

He was a friend.

"You still have that old knack for charming your admirers," Bolan told him wryly.

Anders grinned, shrugged.

"What can I say? It's my magnetic personality."

"You working this officially?"

"Let's call it a fortuitous coincidence. The date was booked, and then it all broke loose between the local Mob and their Eastern competition. Hal figured as long as I'm here, what the hell. . . ."

Mention of the big Fed's name made Bolan smile. The man from Justice was another friend, and friends were few and far between in Bolan's world these days.

"How is... everybody?"

"Getting by. You know how it is—win one here and lose it back over there. You're missed, guy, where it counts." There was a momentary silence and when he resumed the comic's voice was lighter, more upbeat. "I hear you took a turn with Hal there a while back."

Bolan smiled and nodded at the reference. His "turn" had been with a group called Savannah Swingsaw, four women determined to shake up the Mob in the southern United States.

"Some guy," Bolan said.

"Yeah." Another silence, longer this time, finally broken by the comic in a cautious tone. "You here to meet the man from Tokyo?"

"He's on my list. Were those his soldiers at Minotte's?"

"You were there?" Anders's eyes widened briefly. "Well, that clears up some question marks. And the kamikaze squad was his—or a *very* nifty frame."

"There was a girl—"

"Oh, yeah?" The comic raised a lone ironic eyebrow. "I wish you'd tell me where you find the time."

Bolan's answering grin was weary, brief.

"You've got to pace yourself," he answered. "But this was strictly business. Bob Minotte had her in the bag before the samurai express rolled in. I got there just in time to take her out."

"The litter on the highway?"

Anders spoke with mild awe in his voice, a tone that said he knew the answer before Bolan voiced it. The Executioner's silent nod was anticlimactic.

"She does some writing for the *Daily Beacon* here in town. Name's Lucy Bernstein."

A frown creased the ethnician's face. He seemed to be searching for something in the mental data banks and finally found it.

"You don't mean old Abe Bernstein's granddaughter? That the one?"

"Abe Bernstein?"

Small alarms were going off in the back of Bolan's mind, insistent but still ill-defined. The name meant something to him, but. . . .

"You have to know him, man," the comic said. "The Father of Las Vegas. Word is, he built everything that Meyer and Bugsy missed."

And it was coming back to Bolan, sure. He had dismissed the name and face, consigned it to the small "inactive" file reserved for mobsters who retired because of age or illness, but he called the reference back now, ran it through the terminals of memory.

Abe Bernstein was originally from Detroit, where he had helped to found the famous Purple Gang around the time America was entering World War I. He got a jump on Prohibition, staking out a territory on the river just across from Canada and turning bootleg liquor into liquid gold, defending his investment with a formidable army.

A year before Repeal he smelled the winds of change and made the shift from booze to big-time gambling, staking out preserves around Kentucky, Florida and Southern California that saw him through the Great Depression.

When the Mafia started flexing muscle in the thirties, easing out or killing off the old-line Jewish gangsters, Bernstein traveled west, giving ground reluctantly before the Sicilian juggernaut. Along the way he pioneered in legal gaming, setting up his first small clubs in Reno, moving south when Bugsy Siegel struck the mother lode along Las Vegas Boulevard in 1947.

The Gold Rush Hotel–Casino was his first investment in Las Vegas—one of many that included real estate and industry, construction, politics and cattle ranching. Bernstein funneled thousands—some said millions—into local charity and was rewarded with a host of plaques and honors for his labors, testifying to his latter-day respectability.

In time, his sanctuary was invaded once again by mafiosi, and this time there was nowhere to run. As the new wave gradually replaced the old, Abe Bernstein was reduced to something of a puppet, going through the motions of administering that which he once owned outright. Among the Justice Strike Force leaders there was little doubt who held the puppet's strings—and they were long ones, stretching east to Brooklyn and Manhattan.

"I didn't know Abe had a family," Bolan said at last.

The comic frowned.

"A daughter," he responded. "Out of wife number three or four...I don't remember. The daughter's gone now, but there was one child...the granddaughter." Anders hesitated and a chuckle crept into his voice, almost reluctantly. "If she's your Lucy...well, they've got a sense of humor, anyhow."

"What's funny?" Bolan asked.

"Well, Old Jack Goldblume, down there at the *Beacon*...hell, he used to work for Bernstein at the Gold Rush. Handled all the joint's PR back in the old days, before he got religion and went into the civic conscience business full time." Another hesitation and Anders was no longer laughing. "Kind of makes you feel like it's all in the family, eh?"

Bolan barely heard him. He was already thinking through the riddle, trying jumbled pieces, rejecting each in turn and moving on to something new.

Jack Goldblume used to work for Bernstein at the

Gold Rush. Now he ran the *Daily Beacon*, and they were, presumably, still friends.

Now Bernstein's granddaughter—if she *was* his granddaughter—worked for Goldblume. As a plant? A favor for old times' sake?

And Lucy Bernstein, acting under Goldblume's orders, was preparing to expose the very Mafia that owned her grandfather.

Why?

Bolan knew that to receive the necessary answers, he would have to ask the proper questions. And of several potential sources, he planned to start with one who owed him something. Like her life.

12

Bolan found the large apartment complex on the first pass. It was off the main drag two blocks over to the south of West Sahara where he had dropped Lucy Bernstein the night before. A quick call to her number listed in the telephone directory had brought no answer, and the Executioner was betting that last night's festivities had shaken her enough to make her call in sick to work and lay low for a day or two.

As on the previous visit, Bolan found the guard shack out front unattended, and he cruised past, slowing over the omnipresent speed bumps, following the parking lot that ran around the complex proper like an asphalt moat. The buildings fit the martial image, bearing more resemblance to a desert fortress than anything else—white rough stucco with the red tile roofs of vaguely Spanish style.

The soldier parked as close as possible to his intended target, locked the car and left it. Lucy's friend lived back inside the complex, away from the lot, and any way he went about it, he would have to walk. Bolan was counting on the empty sentry booth out front to mean there would be no security on foot inside the complex after nightfall, either.

He passed a combination swimming pool and sauna with a couple hiding from the nighttime chill inside the heated whirlpool bath. Their movements told him they were making love—or maybe only warming up for later—but he did not take the time to stop and check it out. His mind was occupied with war and death at the moment; lovers had no place on Bolan's solitary battlefield.

He moved along the imitation flagstone path to Building 9, then followed his nose around to apartment 186. It was a two-story town house layout and the only lights showing were upstairs, above a boxed-in patio of sorts.

He spent a moment scanning the surroundings, buttoned his jacket shut, and pressed the doorbell set above a cardboard nameplate that identified the occupant.

Feeble chimes inside, then nothing.

Bolan waited thirty seconds and tried again. Now he heard the sound of footsteps on the stairs inside. Despite the muffling distance they sounded heavy, labored. Male.

A light went on behind the French doors to his left, escaping through the peephole in the door. A shadow blocked it out as someone planted an eye against the viewing lens.

"Who is it?" a male voice inquired.

Right, Bolan thought, noting the heavy flavor of the Bronx. Bolan started thinking fast.

"Pizza man."

"We didn't order nothin'."

He played it cautious, knowing this might be a boyfriend of either young woman. He glanced down at an imaginary sales slip in his hand, performing for the benefit of the invisible observer.

And what materialized in his fist was the silenced Beretta 93-R, safety off and ready to rip.

"Well, I gotta note here says deliver one large pepperoni to a Mrs. Castorina," Bolan told the blank impassive door.

There was a hesitation on the other side, slow wheels turning in there and sealing the other man's fate.

"She ain't here now," Mr. Invisible answered. "Must be some mistake."

You made it, slick, the soldier told himself, and plugged a silent mangler through the door six inches underneath the peephole, following through with a kick to the door that exploded the lock mechanism, slamming it back and open, catching the dead man before he had a chance to fall.

Bolan dragged him across the room checking him out with a glance—the scarlet flower blooming on his chest, dead center, and beside him on the floor, a Colt Commander .45 that he would never have another chance to use.

One down.

He scanned the combination living room and kitchen, found it empty. He was moving toward the stairs and homing on the sound of running water when a voice hailed him from the second-floor landing overhead.

More Bronx in this one, with a hint of speech impediment behind the growl.

"Hey, Lenny—what the hell?"

No answer from the leaking Brooklyn delegate.

Bolan waited by the stairs until he heard the sound of cautious footsteps, tracking them halfway down before he made his move, emerging in a combat crouch, the Beretta out in front of him and steadied in both hands.

A chunky goon in shirt-sleeves spent a second gaping at him, finally reaching for the side arm he had stupidly left snug inside its shoulder holster, knowing he could never make it in a million years.

Mack Bolan stroked the trigger twice, and lisping Bronx became a sliding bag of bones, descending gracelessly toward him.

The soldier was already moving, hurdling the corpse and taking the carpeted risers three at a time. The 93-R nosed out ahead of him, and he gained the final landing unopposed.

Two bedrooms opened on his right—both dark, empty. Dead ahead the bathroom door was standing halfway open, spilling pale fluorescent light into the hallway. He heard water running—a bathtub by the sound of it—and Bolan drifted to his right, craning for a better look inside the room.

Another step, and he could see the mirrored medicine cabinet on the wall above a sink. It let him scrutinize the back side of the open door, a towel rack—and the gunner waiting for him just inside.

Bolan stepped back out of sight, approaching catlike and thumbing up the fire-selector switch to shift his weapon from the semiautomatic to 3-shot mode. He took up station three feet from the open door and three feet to its left, directly opposite the waiting gunner, only lath and plaster in between them now.

He held the Beretta up, chest high, imagining the outline of a man emblazoned on the stucco, and stroked the trigger twice, two short bursts ripping through the cheap construction, all six rounds impacting in a fist-sized circle.

A muffled grunt inside was followed by a crash as number three connected face first with the mirrored glass of the medicine cabinet.

Bolan stepped inside and found the gunner wedged between the sink and toilet bowl where he had fallen. His riddled back and lacerated face were dribbling crimson pools that beaded up on contact with the waxed linoleum.

The bathroom's other occupant was stretched out naked in the overflowing tub, her face a precious inch or two above the waterline. And it was Lucy Bernstein, barely alive.

Bolan killed the tap and took a heartbeat to appreciate her beauty before he reached down between the floating legs to pull the plug. He caught her under the arms, lifting the lady up in one fluid motion. When she was clear of the tub, Bolan got an arm beneath her thighs and carried her back past the lifeless *pistolero* to the nearest bedroom.

They might have been interrogating her, but more likely they had meant to kill her and leave it looking like a simple household accident.

Whatever, someone in Minotte's camp had traced her here and, had it not been for Bolan's timely arrival, she would be another colored pin on Captain Reese's wall map.

He left her on the single bed and backtracked to the bathroom for some towels. The lady was alive and Bolan needed answers from her in a hurry. Later he could give thought to searching out a haven in the hellgrounds for her.

Safety was a slim commodity in Vegas, getting more scarce by the moment. Soon there would be no free zones on the battlefield. Before it came to that Bolan had to have some answers. Solutions to the host of problems that were plaguing him, binding his hands in what appeared to be at least a three-way war.

There was the Yakuza with Seiji Kuwahara at the helm, united in a singleness of purpose that could make them deadly in the clenches.

And the Mafia—now anything but solidly united, from the glimpse that Bolan gathered of the meeting at Spinoza's just before he brought the curtain down. If anything, the family representatives seemed likely to attack each other, long before they got around to Kuwahara.

There was the Bernstein faction—if it still existed as an independent entity.

Finally there was Bolan, taking on the world as usual,

with every hand against him in the hellgrounds. The odds were with the house as always, but perhaps, just maybe, he could find the key to trimming down those odds a bit. With good fortune and an assist from the kindly Universe he might even find a way to turn them around for a change.

And there again he needed answers.

Insight.

Truth.

Another scarce commodity in Glitter City—but the Executioner had time to dig for it.

A lifetime, if it came to that.

Perhaps a deathtime.

Either way he was committed—to the end of the line.

13

Bolan gave the woman a brisk rubdown that slowly restored a ruddy color to her body. She started showing signs of life as he was finishing, first coughing, moaning like a trapped and injured animal, finally thrashing out with slender arms and legs in all directions. She had surprising strength—the natural result of desperation. Bolan held her down gently until all resistance ebbed.

When the first defensive spasms passed he brought the sheet and blanket up around her chin, tucking her in like a child. He turned the lights up so that she could see him when she woke, then sat astride a straight-backed chair pulled up beside the bed.

Her eyelids flickered moments later and she looked around, getting her bearings. The eyes settled on Bolan, sparking with recognition, and he was pleased to see her rigid form relax a bit beneath the coverlet.

"It's you...again," she said when she had found her voice.

" 'Fraid so."

She risked a little smile, without conviction.

"Don't be scared. I'm glad to see you."

There was a momentary silence, as she searched the shadows in each corner of the room for any hostile presence.

"The others...."

"They're not with us anymore," he told her simply.

"You...oh, I see."

She was remembering Minotte's more than likely, and the showdown on the highway afterward. He changed the subject, treading softly.

"Where's your roommate?"

"Working nights. She wasn't here when they showed up, thank heaven."

Bolan felt a measure of relief. He had been half expecting to discover yet another female on the premises, this one already cold and stuffed into a cupboard somewhere by the goons before they settled down to handling the main event.

"Okay," he said, "you'll need to warn her off before we leave. Police will have the place sealed off."

"Those men—"

Bolan read the question in the woman's eyes, and answered it forthrightly.

"I don't have time to move them out." He paused, then continued. "Some questions, then we have to get you out of here."

"I understand. I'll make it up to her. . . somehow."

She started to sit up and the covers slipped. Hasty fingers grabbed for the sheet, color flaming her cheeks before she made the save. For the first time Lucy Bernstein seemed to realize that she was naked—and that she had not put herself to bed.

She tried to feign bravado as she spoke to him again, putting a bold face on her obvious embarrassment.

"I guess I don't have many secrets left."

His answer was a thoughtful frown.

"I wouldn't say that."

"Oh?"

She saw that he was serious. Her small self-conscious smile evaporated.

"You said you had some questions?"

Bolan nodded, jumped right into it with both feet.

"How long have you worked for the *Beacon*?"

Lucy looked surprised, taken off guard by his choice of subject matter.

"Going on three years now. I applied right out of journalism school. That's USC," she added, perhaps attempting to impress him.

Bolan was impressed already—by the woman's beauty, by her courage. . . but he was curious about her, too. And he could not afford to take her at face value.

He still needed answers, and he tried a new approach—direct now, sharp.

"I guess the family hookup helped," he said.

She looked confused again.

"What's that supposed to mean?"

He shrugged.

"It means Jack Goldblume and your grandfather go back some forty years. It never hurts to know the boss."

"My grandfather—"

"What do you know about him, really?" Bolan interrupted, silencing her protest.

There was more color in her cheeks, and it was temper now, with no trace of embarrassment. She came up on one elbow, losing the covers again in the process and retrieving them distractedly, her full attention on the nature of Bolan's questioning.

"I know that he's a kindly decent person, Mr. 'Blanski.' Oh, I've heard the stories—all about his whiskey during Prohibition, and the gambling clubs. I know that he was questioned by Congress more than thirty years ago."

She paused, regarding Bolan with a fine hostility, and when she spoke again her tone was almost haughty.

"It's ancient history, my fine self-righteous friend. He's never been indicted, never been convicted—nothing."

"What's that supposed to prove?" he asked her calmly.

She was momentarily speechless and the soldier took advantage of it, veering off along a different track.

"You're working on the Syndicate. I guess you've heard of Frank Spinoza?"

"Certainly."

Her tone was stiff with barely suppressed anger.

"That's Frank Spinoza from New York," he prodded.

"I said I *know* who he is."

But Bolan would not let it go until he made his point.

"Spinoza from New York, who has his office at the Gold Rush."

Lucy was silent now. She watched his face with something close to apprehension in her eyes.

"Your grandfather's casino," Bolan finished. "Jack Goldblume used to run the PR there."

"I know all that," she said. "So what?"

"So, maybe nothing. Maybe I don't buy coincidence."

"You think that my grandfather got me this job?"

Bolan shrugged.

"Well, you're wrong, mister," she snapped. "I'm a damned *good* reporter. There were other offers when I graduated, other opportunities. *I* picked the *Beacon* and Las Vegas. Me. I like it here, okay?"

She was convincing, sure, and Bolan wanted to believe her. But even if she was leveling, it did not mean she knew the full extent of what was going on behind the scenes.

"Who came up with the idea for a Mafia series?" Bolan asked her.

Lucy frowned and somehow it only made her more attractive.

"It just came down," she answered. "I guess the city editor—"

"Or Goldblume?"

She thought about it briefly, nodding.

"Maybe. He's involved in every aspect of the paper. What's the difference?"

Bolan answered her with a question of his own.

"If you were trying to get rid of someone like Minotte or Spinoza, how would you go about it?"

She paled briefly as the memories of last night came flooding back on her again.

"I'd say the Bruce Lee fan club had a fairly workable idea," she said at last.

"Agreed. But let's suppose you're trying to avoid a shooting war. What then?"

"I don't know. Set him up, I guess. Indict him on some charge."

An idea clicked inside the tousled head, and Lucy's mouth was dry when she continued.

"Or you could turn the spotlight on him. Make him vulnerable. . .run him out of town with bad publicity."

"It's worked before," the soldier told her.

She saw where he was going now and did not like it. Verbally, she tried to head him off.

"What's wrong with that?" she challenged. "They *should* be driven out of town."

"I'm less concerned with method than with motive."

"Obviously."

Bolan took the jab for what it was and let it pass, forging ahead in hypotheticals.

"Suppose you had a score to settle, from the old days. Suppose that someone ripped you off years earlier, and now you've got a chance to make it right, with interest."

Lucy Bernstein's voice became indignant.

"This is nonsense. I don't understand—"

"I think you do," he told her softly.

"Well, it doesn't matter what you think. My grandfather. . .Jack Goldblume. . .they're not gangsters like Spinoza. They're both respected businessmen."

He did not answer. In the silence, she continued speaking, and if Bolan read her tone correctly she was trying to persuade herself now.

"Do you know how much money my grandfather gave to charity this year?" she asked him. "Last year? How much Jaćk Goldblume spent on civic service programs?"

"Where'd it all come from, I wonder?"

"God *damn* you!"

"He has," Bolan told her simply, rising from the straight-backed chair and stretching his legs. "You may still have a chance. Get dressed."

"Where are you taking me?" she demanded.

"I've got a friend who specializes in providing sanctuary, more or less official."

There were tears glistening in her eyes, but the voice was tough, unyielding.

"Wait up there, mister. I'm a big girl now. I've got a job, responsibilities—"

A big girl, right, and Bolan did not need to be reminded of the fact.

"You're marked," he told her coldly. "Show up for work with Bob Minotte's family on the hunt, and your next deadline will be just that."

She winced at the play on words and seemed about to answer, but she kept it to herself.

"Get dressed," he said again. "We're out of time."

The clock was running, and Bolan felt the fourth-down pressure without knowing yet exactly what or where his goal might be.

The puzzle was expanding and he had more jumbled jigsaw pieces in his hand.

Lucy Bernstein had a puzzle of her own to deal with now—her own dilemma of the heart and soul. She had some private problems to resolve.

There would not be an easy answer for her, Bolan

knew. But then, a big girl had to live with that reality.

The Executioner had long ago adjusted to the grim reality of living in the hellgrounds. He knew there were no easy answers in the trenches, ever—and no respite from the pressure, either.

He would drop the lady off with Tommy Anders, trust the comic and his people to secure Lucy Bernstein for the duration of his Vegas strike. Whichever way it went, the campaign would be short and decisive. But the intervening time would give Anders a chance to pick her brain a little. Anything he might be able to extract would be a bonus.

As for Bolan, he was already thinking toward the next engagement with an enemy who kept on changing shapes and faces, multiplying. Somewhere soon the answer would walk up to him and tap him on the shoulder. Now, the only problem was that when it came it might be carrying a knife to plant between the Executioner's shoulder blades.

Las Vegas is a city of illusion, and Bolan was not sure that anything he had seen so far was real.

No, scratch that.

He had seen real death, for damn sure. No way to mistake it for show biz make-believe.

He lived in a universe where stark reality was everything. The only avenue of escape from grim relentless truth was a parabellum mangler through the brain.

And he resided in the charnel universe by choice, damn right. Along with others like Brognola and Tommy Anders—the combatants who elected to spend their season in hell here on earth.

No one had drafted warrior Bolan for this holy war. He had elected to provide his body and his soul, a living sacrifice.

But Lucy Bernstein....

She was something else again.

A big girl, right, who might not get much older if allowed to wander pell-mell through the battlefields of Bolan's war. Accustomed to the newsroom she was unfamiliar with the no-rules rules of war, and there was no damned time to train her in the martial arts that she would need to eke out a survival in the trenches.

Let the woman find her peace or purgatory in her own way, her own time. Mack Bolan had already found his course of action and he was proceeding with it, undeterred and undetoured by any of Glitter City's myriad distractions.

There were lots of big girls out there, right.

And there were lots of big *guns*, too.

Right now most of them were not aimed at Bolan, but the coming hours would change all that. The Executioner was counting on it.

14

Frank Spinoza finished loading the clip for his Browning Hi-Power automatic pistol and snapped it into the pistol grip, working the weapon's slide to chamber up a live one. He eased down the hammer and set the safety, enjoying the weight of the loaded gun in his hand.

Reluctantly he reached out to stow it in the top desk drawer, then reconsidered, slipping it inside the waistband of his slacks, on the left, where it was hidden underneath his jacket.

The solid weight of it felt good there against his ribs.

For the first time since that afternoon Spinoza felt secure, sitting there behind his massive desk inside the private office.

The gun was part of it, he knew. And the layout of the office helped.

No windows.

He had been expecting Paulie Vaccarelli's knock, and even so, it made him jump involuntarily. Spinoza gripped the padded arms of his swivel chair, willing himself to relax with an effort.

"Come ahead," he ordered.

The houseman stepped inside, the door ajar behind him and his body sealing off the opening. His rugged face seemed out of balance now with a bulky bandage on his cheek across the wound he received from flying window glass.

Spinoza wondered if he would ever stand before

another open window totally at ease, without feeling fear in the pit of his stomach.

Paulie's voice cut through his private thoughts, a welcome interruption at the moment.

"Abe's here."

Spinoza cleared his throat to rout the squeak.

"Okay. Thanks, Paulie."

The houseman backed out and a moment later Abe Bernstein entered. To Spinoza he was moving like a little boy expecting trouble from his grade-school principal. Hell, everyone knew it must have been a hundred frigging years since Bernstein was in school.

He looked like some cartoonist's notion of Methuselah, standing there impassively watching Frank through his wire-rimmed spectacles.

Spinoza did not know exactly how old Bernstein was—a very cautious estimate would place him somewhere in his early eighties—but whatever it was, he looked his age. The thinning hair was frosty white and Bernstein's tailored suit could not disguise the thickening around his waist, the slight droop to his shoulders. He still carried himself pretty well for his age, but the years had carved deep furrows in his face beneath the sunlamp tan and added on some surplus chins.

The old man used to be some kind of hot shit in his day, when it was booze from Canada that brought the bucks instead of grass from Mexico and coke from South America. The frigging Purple Gang, for crying out loud. What was that, some kind of Jewish ethnic humor?

Spinoza felt like laughing to himself. Those bad-assed Jews had ruled the roost around Detroit—until they ran into the Brotherhood. It did not take them long to cut and run when they came face-to-face with bold and bad Sicilians.

Purple Gang, my ass, Spinoza thought. More like the Yellow Gang.

And where were they now? Filling bone orchards back east, most of them. A few survivors had retired into obscurity or lived, like Bernstein, on the sufferance of the Brotherhood. Manhattan owned Abe Bernstein—body, soul, and diamond pinky ring—the whole nine yards.

Spinoza broke the silence, speaking as he would to a subordinate, his voice and manner vaguely condescending.

"Abe, I need your help."

"Whatever I can do," the old man answered.

"We've got some company coming in. A lot of company. They're landing at McCarran in . . . oh—" he made a show of consulting his Rolex "—let's call it ninety minutes."

Spinoza met the old man's eyes and dropped his bomb.

"They're going to need some rooms."

"How many?" Bernstein asked.

"All of 'em."

Abe's smile faltered, freezing at half-mast.

"You're joking, right?"

Spinoza shook his head, eyes never leaving Bernstein's face.

"I've never been more serious."

That did it for the smile. Old Abe was glowering at him now across the desk.

"It's Friday night. We're almost full, Frank."

"So?"

"So, that's three hundred fifty rooms with paying guests. We can't put all those people on the street. You can't need *all* those rooms."

Spinoza shrugged, enjoying the game now.

"You're right. They'll only need a third of that. Fact is, I want an empty house."

A hesitation, Bernstein judging just how far he dared go.

"Why's that, Frank?"

Spinoza allowed himself a frown although he felt like laughing in the old man's face.

"I don't owe you any explanations, Abe. But since you ask, our visitors are going to need their privacy."

He paused, dragging it out to get the maximum effect from his pronouncement.

"It's a head party, Abe. We're going hard."

"I see."

His tone informed Spinoza very clearly that he did not like it. Which was fine. The old man did not have a vote in the proceedings.

"That make you nervous, Abe?" Spinoza asked, toying with him now.

Bernstein shook his snowy head.

"I'm old," he said. "I don't get nervous, Frank. I just get tired."

"Well, save your strength, old man. I'm gonna need you here to man the fort until this thing blows over."

There was weary resignation in his voice as Bernstein answered.

"Anything you say, Frank."

"Good."

"What should I tell our guests? Where are they going to go?"

"I don't care what you tell them. Use your own imagination—union problems, broken plumbing...anything. Just get them out. I'm calling in some markers on the Strip to get the rooms we need. We'll have it covered by the time you get them packed."

"The transportation—"

"Is no problem, Abe," Spinoza interrupted him, and he was getting irritated now. The game was over. "They don't have wheels, we'll run the limos, stick 'em on the damn bus—who cares? Don't make a problem out of nothing.''

''Right.''

''We're set, then?''

''Set.'' The old man nodded confirmation.

''Okay, get on it.''

Abe Bernstein let himself out of the private office, and Spinoza was left alone. At once the mafioso put him out of mind, already moving on to other more important things. The old man would do what he was told—or he would rue the consequences of his failure.

In the coming hours Frank Spinoza would command an army, finally get his chance to move against the common enemy. A tardy move, no question there, but not *too* late.

Not yet.

The troops had been reluctantly provided subsequent to his last conversation with The Man. New York was still opposed to open warfare in the city, but as long as it was unavoidable, as long as someone else had started it, at least they meant to win.

His own accounting of the sniper raid and Julio DePalma's grisly end had turned the trick. Spinoza was convinced of it. The old oratorical gift coming through for him again as it always had in the past.

He had sensed that many different ears were listening to him as he laid it out—perhaps the whole Five Families—and he had spared them nothing on the scrambled line. He let them see poor Julio—the bastard, coming at Spinoza that way—splattered on the walls and leaking out his life into the deep-shag carpet. And the others, flopping, dying. . . .

When he had finished, New York asked him what he needed. No more waiting, no more arguments, no stalling. Just a blank check with a single string attached.

He had to make it good and make it fast.

If he should fumble somehow. . . .

No.

Spinoza put the thought out of his mind. Defeat was out of the question.

He had a chance to show the powers that be another side of Frank Spinoza here tonight. And let them see that he could hold his own in battle, not just in the peace negotiations afterward.

If—no—*when* he pulled it off, he would be in a position to dictate some rather different terms. Perhaps to cut himself a hefty slice of the pie.

Spinoza eased the Browning from his belt and set it on the desk in front of him, its muzzle pointed at the office door. He was looking forward to the opportunity of using it. Tonight, perhaps. Tomorrow for certain. If the campaign lasted any longer. . . .

Spinoza smiled to himself, his mind at ease now. Seiji Kuwahara had already missed his chance. Pearl Harbor, hell. It would be frigging Hiroshima and Nagasaki all rolled into one before he finished with the little yellow bastard.

And he meant to plant him personally.

The future capo of Las Vegas owed it to himself.

15

The white phone caught Brognola halfway out the office door. He thought about ignoring it but habit and a sense of duty drew him back.

He did not bother turning on the lights. The big Fed knew his office like he knew the inside of his home, and he navigated around the lurking obstacles to reach the desk, lifting the receiver on the fifth ring.

"Go."

It was a private line reserved for use by agents in the field. The SOG line, every bit as vital to Bolan as the other one that terminated in the Oval Office. Each line without the other formed a broken circuit.

Brognola was the link between them, joining them into a working whole—and that meant he was constantly on call.

"I ran into a friend of ours out here tonight," the caller told him.

He recognized the voice of Tommy Anders instantly. "Out here" was Vegas, naturally. As for the rest of it—

"We don't have any friends out there," he answered gruffly.

"Well, maybe one," the comic amended.

"I don't follow you, Joker."

The big Fed felt a familiar sour burning in his stomach. Hell, he thought he had *that* cured. He was lying to the operative, sure...and to himself. He had been getting bulletins from Vegas through the day, and now Brognola knew exactly who the "friend out there" must be.

Mack Bolan, right.

The hellfire guy was out there, living on the edge as always, cutting through the bureaucratic bull in his search for essence.

And Brognola could envy him that, his dramatic successes, even as he mourned a sense of loss inside himself.

The comic's voice demanded his attention, small and far away.

"Maybe you can follow this, then." Anders sounded irritated, shifting into flat-out anger. "Our boy's between a hammer and the anvil here. Could be two hammers, if his latest hunch pans out."

A moment's hesitation, and the angry voice was somewhat softer when it spoke again.

"He could use some help, man."

"Sorry, he's not our boy anymore."

There was something in Brognola's throat all of a sudden, threatening to choke him, and he put a hand across the mouthpiece, coughing hard to clear it.

"Dammit, Hal!"

"Dammit, nothing," Brognola snapped back. "Striker . . . made his choice. He'll have to live with it."

"Or die with it?"

"He knows the risks, Joker. Hell, he wrote the book."

"It could be someone's tacking on a whole new chapter while he isn't looking."

Brognola frowned. He did not want to hear this, but he could not shut the comic off without allowing him to finish his report. He would just have to take the information for whatever it was worth, divorce himself from Bolan's side of it entirely.

If he could.

If not. . . .

"So, let me have it, Joker."

"The name of Bernstein ring a bell?"

"You don't mean Leonard?"

"Let's try Abe, for starters."

"That's old business."

"Maybe . . . maybe not."

Brognola did not like the feeling that was creeping up his spine and sliding icy tendrils out along his scalp.

"What's the rumble?"

Anders cleared his throat and started fresh.

"Striker thinks the old-boy network may be working out some kind of end run on the families out here."

"Where does Tokyo come into it?" Brognola asked him.

"Could be a wild card, a diversion—take your pick. Whatever hassles Frank Spinoza and the rest of them is good for business, right? Our guy's not sure on that point yet."

"He's not—"

"Our guy," the comic finished for him. "Sure. All right, already. You can't blame a guy for trying."

"No, I can't at that."

"So how about it?"

"What?"

Brognola knew what Anders wanted from him, but he stubbornly refused to openly acknowledge it.

"You *know* what. When can we expect the cavalry?"

"No cavalry on this one, Joker. I had too much explaining to do the last time I helped him. Not to mention the cost in personal suffering." Brognola grimaced as the burning pain lanced his stomach. "You're observing, and that's all. If anybody tries some independent action—"

"Then we leave him hanging out there on his own. That it?"

"That's it," Brognola told him leadenly. "He knew the game plan when he bought his ticket."

Stony silence on the other end and Hal Brognola lasted all of ninety seconds with the frostbite gnawing at his ear.

"Okay, I'll make some calls, goddammit. See what I can do. Don't count on anything."

"I never do. But thanks."

The line went dead and Brognola hung it up at his end. He pulled a cigar from the inside pocket of his coat and fired the stogie up, drawing acrid smoke deep down into his lungs.

The doctors had been telling him to cut down on his smokes, or give them up entirely, but sometimes they were the only thing that helped him to relax, to think a problem through.

Like now.

Mack Bolan was in Vegas. Naturally.

There was trouble in Nevada, with a Mob war brewing. And where else would the hellfire warrior be but right there in the middle of it all.

Nowhere else.

Brognola missed the guy and grieved for him as if the Executioner was dead already. He had slipped beyond the pale when he bailed out of the official Phoenix program. When it came down to offering assistance to an outlaw.

Like the old days. When Bolan was the world's most wanted fugitive with a price on his head from both sides of the law.

Small world, for damned sure, and it just kept turning, bringing everything around full circle in the end. Sometimes it seemed to Brognola that the past few years had never happened, that he was right back where he started from the first time that he heard Mack Bolan's name.

But that was wrong, and when the momentary anger passed he realized the error in his thinking.

They were long miles down the road from where they had started out together, and they had scored some touchdowns for the right side on the way. The world might not be different to the naked eye, but if you strained your vision, underneath the smog bank were some clean spots, which Brognola and the Executioner had scrubbed free of their slime.

The cleanser they had used was every bit as old as man himself. Fire and blood, in equal mixture, with a lot of elbow grease thrown in to make it bite down hard and deep.

They had made changes and scored some victories that no one could deny—albeit largely classified and buried in some filing cabinet somewhere.

They had been good together and the remnants of the Phoenix Project stood as a memorial to their achievement.

Not that Hal was patting himself on the back, hell no. He did not have the interest or, at almost midnight on a Friday, the energy.

He was convincing himself, applying the fine art of interior persuasion. Psyching himself up to do what he knew must be done in spite of all the orders and regulations to the contrary.

He meant to help Mack Bolan if he could. And that was far from certain given his surroundings, the hour . . . a whole host of variables beyond his control.

But he would try.

Because he had to.

The Executioner was out there. Still living large. Still fighting. *Their* fight.

And so what if he was not "our guy" anymore?

He would be Hal Brognola's guy as long as the big Fed could draw breath and stand up on his own size thirteens.

Brognola settled down behind his desk with weary resignation, dragged the telephone across to him and started making calls.

Tommy Anders sat on the edge of his hotel bed, staring at the silent telephone. He tried to think of someone he could call, of something he could say—and every time it wound up in a ghastly gallows-humor parody.

Hello, Clark County Sheriff? FBI? Whoever? This is Tommy Anders calling from the Sultan's Lounge. That's right. Well, since you ask, I'm calling to report a gang war. Oh, you heard? Well, does the name Mack Bolan ring a bell?

He shook his head disgustedly. Brognola would do everything he could, the comic knew that, but it might not be enough. And he was rankled by the Fed's reluctance to assist a man who had done so much for the cause. If there was only something—

Of course there was.

Bolan had entrusted him with Lucy Bernstein and he could keep her safe and sound until the storm blew over. He could take that load off Bolan's shoulders, right— and in the process, he could try to get some information out of her.

Anders was not sure he followed Bolan's logic on that business with the old-boy network. Anything was possible, of course, but it was hard to visualize a bunch of grizzled old-timers taking on the new breed of the Mafia. At first glance it was like the plot of some peculiar cops-and-robbers sitcom—"The Revenge of the Over-the-Hill Gang," dammit.

Except that Bolan was not laughing when he spelled it out for Tommy Anders.

He was deadly serious and that was good enough to wipe the smile off Tommy's face for starters. Whether anybody else was buying it or not the comic was convinced that Bolan's theory merited a closer scrutiny. And if his hunch was anywhere near being on the money....

Then what?

What if old Abe Bernstein and his cronies were committed to a course of putting heat on Frank Spinoza and the rest of them through media exposure? Anders frowned. There would be more, much more to it than that, he knew.

The geriatric crowd had never hatched a single altruistic thought among themselves—and likely never would. If they were going up against the Mafia now—headlines, in the streets, whatever—they would ha' motive more or less commensurate with risk.

And he was back at the initial question once again.

What motive?

Good old everyday revenge would do for openers. The Mafia had looted Bernstein's castle, relegated him to puppet status, and the same had happened to number of his close confederates.

Revenge, if he read it right. Still, it was not enough. The Mafia had made its move on Bernstein and the others nearly thirty years ago. If they were going to make a move—

He gave it up. The sterile exercise was getting him nowhere...and he was wasting time.

The woman with the answers—some of them at any rate—was waiting for him just beyond the bedroom door. He had required some privacy for his communication with Brognola, but the time had come to see exactly what she knew.

If anything.

And Tommy Anders knew exactly how to go about it He was an expert. Wit and charm would do the trick.

"Well, now—"

He froze in the open bedroom doorway, instantly forgetting everything he planned to say. He would not need it now.

There was nobody left to say it to.

The woman had slipped out on him while he was on the line to Wonderland.

"Goddammit!"

He had kissed off his one and only chance to lend a hand in Bolan's desert war. His chance was gone, the woman was gone...and only open-ended questions lingered on.

Where had she gone?

And why?

If it was lack of trust in Anders, Lucy's urge to find a haven of her own, they had no problem. But if she had run to grandpa, say, or to Jack Goldblume, telling tales. . . .

She knew who Bolan was; the comic felt it in his gut although no words had passed between them in his presence that would make it firm. He got it from the way she looked at Bolan, listened to him as if she was trying to remember every word for future reference.

She could be trouble, no doubt about it. Even if she went directly to the law or to her Wang terminal with the story, rather than to Grandpa Abe, she could be signing Bolan's death certificate.

"Dammit!"

And again, with feeling.

"*Damn* it!"

Tommy Anders did not like the helpless feeling, but he knew that he had played his only ace already. If Hal Brognola and his troops could not help Bolan, there was nothing that a stand-up comic could accomplish on his own.

The greatest solitary player of them all was out there on the streets already, carrying the fire for all of those who had to stand by watching helplessly. With any luck at all, his martial skills and sheer audacity would be enough.

America's ethnician reached the bar in three long strides and found himself a fifth of rye. He had already called in "sick" for the remainder of the evening and his replacement would be well into the second show by now. As for Tommy Anders, he was settling down to have a drink or two—or ten—and keeping watch along the home front.

He only hoped it would not be a death watch for the Executioner.

16

"Come on, we haven't got much time," Abe Bernstein said agitatedly. "Let's wrap it up."

The three of them were meeting in his office at the Gold Rush. It was risky, but his two companions were familiar faces in the hotel and casino. They could pass unnoticed in the mounting chaos going on outside his door, and it was safer now to have them visit him in person than to talk their business on the phones, which Frank Spinoza would no doubt be monitoring.

They were relatively safe for the moment, but Abe Bernstein still felt a sense of urgency. He had delegated much of his responsibility in clearing out the Gold Rush to his underlings, but he would have to let himself be seen around the premises or run the risk of bringing down suspicion on himself.

And that, at this precarious stage, could be disastrous.

Across the desk from Bernstein, his companions had the air of generals on the eve of an invasion—confident, but with a sort of tension, an expectancy about them that was thinly veiled.

Jack Goldblume, patriarch of the Las Vegas *Daily Beacon* and a friend for over forty years, was slender, seventy, and looking fit from daily workouts in his private gym. And, Bernstein knew, from private workouts with a sleek succession of young would-be show girls in his bedroom.

Decades after they were separated in a widely celebrated falling-out, old Jack was still his good right hand, still handling the press whenever Bernstein needed a kind word—or a gaff delivered to his enemies.

The media would play a crucial role across the next few hours and days as all the pieces fell into their designated slots. Abe Bernstein meant his version of the story to be first out on the wire; whatever followed would be running second best.

On Goldblume's right sat Harry Thorson, bearing strong resemblance to a troll decked out in Western gear, with patterned sequins on his jacket and a snake-skin band encircling his roll-brim Stetson. His face was deeply tanned, like ancient saddle leather, with a paler knife scar staggering from the corner of his right eye to the jowl, now flabby and gone soft with time.

A Texas native, Thorson came to Vegas close behind Abe Bernstein in the forties. Texan lawmen sought his extradition on a range of charges that included homicide, extortion and a host of others. But strategic contributions to the reelection efforts of an understanding governor had kept him safe and sound inside Nevada while the statutes ran and legal deadlines passed unnoticed. The Alamo Casino, down the gulch from Bernstein's Gold Rush, was a living monument to Thorson's gratitude; the understanding governor, retired now, and a host of relatives were permanently on the payroll.

The aging cowboy still had muscle in Las Vegas and up north, around the capital at Carson City. They would have need of those political connections soon, before the battlesmoke had settled in Las Vegas.

"The PR's covered, Abe," Jack Goldblume said. "Whichever way it goes—"

"It better only go *one* way, Jack," Harry Thorson interjected.

"It'll go," Abe Bernstein told them both. "I've got

our people on the job already. When New York checks in, we'll help them feel at home."

"That's some room service," Thorson chortled. "Tuck 'em in and put their ass to sleep. I love it."

Goldblume shifted uneasily in his chair.

"We have to be especially careful," he reminded no one in particular. "I can keep a lid on what goes down inside here—*maybe* I can keep the lid on—but if anything slops over to the streets. . . ."

"Don't give yourself an ulcer, Jack. Let's take it as it comes." Bernstein turned to Harry Thorson. "What's the word from Carson City?"

Thorson shrugged.

"Whispers, rumbles—you know the route. No one's gonna miss Spinoza or the rest of them, but natcherly they can't come out and say so for the record. If Frankie and his crew should turn up missing—well, I get the feeling that there won't be any posses tearin' up the countryside to find 'em."

Thorson's message was not lost on Bernstein. The law could not assist them, but it would not interfere as long as it could look the other way discreetly.

And Abe Bernstein was the soul of discretion.

"Fair enough," he said. "We'll have to clean it up ourselves, and keep it clean."

"How many guns they bringin' in?" Harry asked.

Bernstein shrugged distractedly. "I haven't got a head count yet. Let's figure somewhere in the neighborhood of fifty."

Goldblume whistled softly to himself. "That's an army," he said.

Bernstein raised a curious eyebrow.

"Getting nervous, Jack?" he asked.

Goldblume turned indignant. "Hell, no. I just hate to see it come so far and then run out of steam."

"We're ready, Jack. Believe it. You just mind the headlines and stand clear."

"Sure, Abe, I just thought—"

"Don't think, Jack. It'll get you into trouble."

Goldblume looked hurt and Bernstein quickly moved to salve his old friend's wounded feelings.

"Listen, I'll be counting on your series to provide the background for some sudden disappearances. You up for it?"

The newsman nodded, making a show of self-assurance.

"Another day or two, at most—the Sunday supplement, for sure. We'll have it on the stands before Spinoza and the others turn up missing."

"Fine. We'll let the locals give you credit for a cleaner Vegas."

"What about New York? Chicago?" Goldblume asked. "Those boys won't take it lying down."

Abe Bernstein's voice turned hard as tempered steel.

"Then let 'em take it bending over." Harry Thorson chuckled appreciatively as Abe pushed ahead. "Once we have the town sewed up, they'll all be on the outside, looking in. They don't have guts enough to kill the golden goose. We're sitting on the biggest gold mine in the country. If they want a little piece of what we've got, they'd better ask real nice."

"Forget the nice," Thorson interjected. "They better get down on their goddamn knees and *beg*."

Abe Bernstein smiled. They were together once again, the shadow-doubts defeated, driven back into a corner. He checked his watch.

"I've gotta shake a leg. You both know what to do?"

"No sweat," the cowboy answered. "It's in the bag, Abe."

Bernstein glanced at Goldblume, received a jerky nod of confirmation.

"Well, then, let's get on it. I've got a plane to meet."

They all rose, and he shook the hand of each man in turn.

"I'll see you back here for the main event?"

"Damn right," Thorson beamed. "I wouldn't miss it."

"I'll be here," Goldblume promised, but he sounded considerably less enthused than Thorson by the prospect.

Bernstein saw them out and closed the office door behind them. He would give them time to clear the premises before he made another round to supervise the mass evacuation under way. No point in taking any chances, with victory so close now that he could taste it.

He was concerned about Jack Goldblume. All those years behind a desk had taken something out of him—the old vitality, the nerve. Perhaps when they were finished Jack would get it back. If not....

Well, newsmen were expendable.

And old friends?

Yes. Them, too.

Abe Bernstein was about to realize a dream he had been cherishing for thirty years and more. Revenge required precision planning and the father of Las Vegas had devoted three decades to winning back the empire that was rightly his. Spinoza and his kind had ruled the roost for too damn long already. It was time for them to settle up their debts.

In blood.

He was ready to unleash a crimson river on the streets—a desert flash flood that would sweep the city clean of that Italian scum. *His* city, sure—and never mind Jack Goldblume's seeming lack of nerve. If they were able to contain their action at the Gold Rush, fine. If not—no matter. Bernstein did not seek publicity, by any means, but if it came....

He was the father of Las Vegas, dammit, and he had the right—the bounden *duty*—to defend the city he had done so much to build. The people of Las Vegas—his people—would salute him if they knew what he was doing.

He was cleaning up Las Vegas and if he should turn a profit in the process...well, so much the better. It was the American way, and who was more deserving than himself?

He was a goddamn civic hero. They owed him something, all of them, for what he had accomplished—and for what he was about to do.

Especially that.

He was disposing of the Mafia, relieving Vegas of a plague. And later, when the dust had settled, he would deal with Seiji Kuwahara and his Eastern imports, too.

First the plague and then the yellow fever.

Bernstein chuckled to himself feeling better already, younger than he had in years. He had been working toward this moment all his life, and now that it was here the savior of Las Vegas knew that he was ready.

Abe Bernstein left his office, moving eagerly to meet the future that was waiting for him.

17

Lucy Bernstein slipped a twenty to the cabbie as she disembarked a block short of the Gold Rush entrance. Limousines stood two deep at the curb, obstructing traffic regally, and Lucy spied a charter bus idling on the nearest side street.

The sidewalk all around the bus and limousines was clotted with a press of tourists dragging luggage, red-coated bellboys weaving in among them, offering assistance where they could and pocketing the rare last-chance gratuities.

She made her way upstream against the human current, finally gained the glass revolving doors and spent another moment jostling faceless strangers, being shoved and elbowed more than once before she made it to the lobby proper.

Inside, the hotel lobby was a larger replay of the sidewalk scene she had just witnessed. Ranks of angry guests were crowding up against the registration desk, all jabbering in unison at two beleaguered clerks, demanding refunds, glowering at the promises of other rooms in comparable hotels. One of the patrons, florid faced and beefy in a garish flowered shirt, had to be restrained by uniformed security from hurdling the counter and extracting his deposit from the cash drawer.

Lucy veered away from the confusion, almost colliding with a Kansas-farmer type, his wheat-blond wife and stair-step children strung out single file behind him, all intent on plowing through the crowd toward freedom and the street outside. She moved across the lobby, searching for her grandfather amid the chaos.

Fifteen minutes passed before she spotted him. She saw his white hair bobbing like a fleck of sea foam on the surging human tide. He moved with easy self-assurance through the crush—here speaking gently to an agitated guest, there giving orders to an employee. Lucy approached him, reaching out to touch him on the shoulder.

He turned to face her, smiling—and she saw the plasticized expression falter for an instant as he made the recognition. He took her by the arm and steered her in the direction of his office.

"Lucy...what on earth...! What brings you out here on a night like this?"

"Like what?" she asked. "What's going on around here, grandpa?"

Bernstein spread his hands and smiled expansively.

"We're looking at some trouble with the culinary workers. Some damn thing about the pension plan. They're walking out at midnight, and we're putting up our guests at other places till it all blows over."

Lucy was confused.

"A wildcat strike? I haven't heard a thing about it at the paper."

"It came at us out of nowhere. Who can figure unions?"

They had reached the office and he ushered her inside. The closing door cut off the babble from the lobby.

"So, Lucy, would you like a soft drink? Or some wine?" He looked embarrassed. "I keep forgetting that you're not a little girl."

"No, thanks."

"Well, then...what can I do for you?"

She was hesitant now, nervous, having second thoughts about her presence at the Gold Rush.

"If you're too busy now.... I could come back another time."

"Too busy for my one and only grandchild. Never, Lucy. Tell me what you need."

"Some answers, grandpa."

He smiled, but with a hint of caution now.

"Ah. The journalist."

"I don't know how to ask you this...."

"The simplest way is usually best. So, ask."

"How well do you know Frank Spinoza?"

"Frank?"

Did she imagine the surprise behind his eyes, the ripple of uneasiness that spread like fleeting pallor underneath his sunlamp tan?

No. It was there.

"We work together, Lucy," he was saying. "You know that. I guess you'd say I work *for* him."

"I've always wondered how that happened, grandpa. I mean, how Spinoza wound up running the hotel and everything you built from scratch."

Another flicker there behind the slick facade, but quickly hidden now, before she had a chance to name it.

"These things happen, Lucy. Businessmen run into trouble.... Spinoza and his people helped me out, and in return I got myself some partners."

"Who exactly are Spinoza's people?"

"Eastern businessmen, some bankers, some—"

He hesitated, spread his hands and shook his head.

"I'm not about to tell you lies. Some of them... well...you hear these stories. Truth is, there are stories people tell about your grandpa, too, from the old days."

Lucy could not meet his eyes now. When she answered him her voice was soft, subdued.

"I've heard them."

"So?" He ruffled fingers through his snowy hair.

"You see the horns? Smell brimstone? Lucy, every man has done some things he's not too proud of. Maybe if I had the chance to go back fifty, sixty years, I'd do some things a little differently."

He hesitated, pinned her with a searching stare.

"I can't go back, Luce. Nobody can. What's done is done."

"And what's about to happen?"

He frowned.

"Now you're talking riddles."

"Grandpa, there are stories...rumors.... Are you planning something?"

"Something? Lucy—"

"With Frank Spinoza? Or against him...I don't know...."

His voice was on the razor's edge of anger when he spoke again.

"Who filled your head with this *meshugeneh* idea?"

"It doesn't matter, grandpa."

"Well...what would I do to Frank Spinoza? What could I do?"

"I'm sorry, really. I don't know...."

"Forget about it, Lucy. I understand how these things sound sometimes."

"I'd better let you go. You've got your hands full here."

She was having trouble keeping tears out of her voice now as she turned toward the office door. She wanted to be out of there, away from him. The destination did not matter to her, just as long as she was moving.

"You stop by any time," he told her. "And never be afraid to ask me anything, Lucy. Anything at all."

"I love you, grandpa."

But she could not face him. Could not let him have the parting kiss that they had always shared from childhood.

"Lucy—"

But she was already moving, the noises of the crowded lobby closing in around her, drowning out the old man's words. The tears were in her eyes now, burning, threatening to spill across her cheeks. The ache inside her chest was so intense she felt that it might steal her breath away.

He had been lying to her, with the ease of endless practice. He had been lying, start to finish. Lucy knew it in her heart, and with the knowledge came a stabbing pain that pierced her like an ice pick.

There had not been a wildcat strike in Vegas for as long as Lucy could remember; they were clearing out the Gold Rush for some other reason. But why? To accommodate whom?

And what about Spinoza? Every answer dealing with the New York mafioso had been just a shade too easy somehow. None of them rang true.

As if in answer to her secret thoughts, she recognized the face of Frank Spinoza across the crowded lobby. He was standing near the main security station, deep in conversation with another man she did not recognize—until he turned sideways.

Lucy placed the profile in a single lurching heartbeat.

He was one of the hoodlums who had viewed her in captivity at Minotte's and briefly listened in on her interrogation by the boss before the roof collapsed around them.

And what would he be doing with Spinoza? Were New York and Chicago joining hands somehow? And did their business help explain the sudden mass evacuation of the Gold Rush in the dead of night?

Her tears were dry as Lucy Bernstein slowed her pace, no longer heading for the exit and the crowded sidewalk now, but drifting in the general direction of Spinoza and his company. The two of them were moving toward the bank of elevators, with another pair of flashy suits in tow. Lucy fell in step a cautious distance to the rear.

Her news sense drove her now. She was determined to uncover what the man she trusted most in all the world before tonight was so determined to conceal.

She meant to follow Frank Spinoza and his trail of slime wherever they might lead, and in the end, if some of his corruption should rub off on others—on her grandfather—well, she would deal with that when she came to it.

The man had made his choice years before she was born, and he could live with it—as she would live with what she had to do that night. She had no choice.

Lucy Bernstein had a duty, and she would see it through, no matter what the cost. There was no turning back from this point even if it killed her.

And it might, she knew with sudden chilling clarity.

ABE BERNSTEIN WATCHED his granddaughter cross the crowded lobby, finally losing sight of her before she reached the registration desk and exit. He tried to put her out of mind but he could not dismiss her questions quite so easily.

She had been fencing with him, but why? That business with Spinoza had been too damned close for comfort, and he wondered where she heard the rumors of their troubles. No one knew the plan outside of his immediate organization. If they had a leak at this late date....

Bernstein calmed himself with an effort. He was building problems out of nothing now, he knew. She must have been uncovering bits and pieces for the series Goldblume had assigned her to—the one that was supposed to break on Sunday. It was inevitable that his name would surface in the course of her inquiry—he had built the goddamned Gold Rush, after all—and he could stand the heat, the trace of accusation in her eyes where only childlike love and trust had shown before.

He hoped she was not getting too immersed in all this Mafia business. It was a fading brotherhood though Frank Spinoza did not know it yet. They needed the cover Lucy's series would provide, but it was only that. She did not have to know the ending. Abe intended to write that for himself, beginning very shortly.

He moved across the crowded lobby, smiling absent-mindedly and receiving mostly hostile stares in answer. He was halfway to the wide casino concourse when a husky bellboy flagged him down, appearing to continue with his futile sweeping while they spoke.

"We're set," the bellhop told him, dark eyes scanning cautiously around the lobby.

"All right. They're due within the hour. We'll be waiting for a clear shot. No one makes a move without my word."

"You've got it."

He moved along, secure that everything was ready.

The sweeper was one of Bernstein's "specials," hand-picked with an eye toward ruggedness and military backround. There were forty of them on the premises this night, each one with weapons on his person or within his reach, all prepared to make their move on Bernstein's word.

It was a private strike force primed for action, with Abe Bernstein's finger on the trigger.

He had taken pains in the selection of his commandos, gleaning out the best available from mercenary sources over eighteen months of careful shopping. He had supervised their training personally, hiding them among a crop of young Olympic hopefuls working out at the exclusive health spa that he owned in Southern California.

Procurement of their arms, the final honing of their

lethal skills in combat situations, was accomplished in conjunction with the neo-fascist paramilitary gangs who populate the Southern California desert with their training camps and arsenals.

Forty soldiers, right—each finely tuned and with a special duty to perform when Bernstein gave the signal. Teams to close the hotel off from outside access, others for the hotel wings, prepared to move from room to room until they had eliminated every Eastern gunner. More to handle any stragglers in the restaurant and lobby area, making it a clean sweep.

When Bernstein gave the word, they would transform the Gold Rush briefly into the biggest morgue in town.

But not just yet.

He had to wait until the final guests were bussed away to alternate hotels, their places taken by gorillas who were circling McCarran Airport at that very moment.

When everyone was present and accounted for—the imports and Spinoza's coterie of shaky allies on the local front—then Bernstein would be ready to unleash his strike force. And he was looking forward to it with relish.

There was a great day coming for Las Vegas—and for Bernstein. He was about to do a favor on behalf of justice. Poetic justice.

And it was going to be a pleasure.

18

Frank Spinoza took his time about emerging from the elevator. He would be at a disadvantage if he seemed too eager, too uncertain of himself. He could not afford to let the new arrivals think that he was unable to hold down his end. He had to deal from strength or they might find a way to ease him out along with Kuwahara's kamikazes.

Spinoza watched as the first contingent of arrivals from the East grouped up around the entrance, waiting for the porters to unload their bags. Outside, the rest were quickly piling out of airport limos, unwilling to expose themselves on hostile soil until they knew the layout.

Spinoza planned to let them get their fill of action as soon as possible, but first he had to play the role of host to the assembled hunters.

The lobby was a wasteland now, devoid of paying guests, with only Bernstein's few employees and the new arrivals. The place was deathly quiet—calm before the storm—and Frank Spinoza realized how much he missed the jangle of casino action from the big adjacent room. Right now, without the players his casino was lifeless—like a tomb.

Spinoza pushed the morbid image out of mind and crossed the lobby, Paulie Vaccarelli trailing at his elbow. Time enough to get the players back when he had dealt with Kuwahara and the frigging Yakuza once and for all.

Spinoza was a dozen paces out when one of the Manhattan soldiers peeled away and moved to greet him, two more falling in behind but hanging back a yard or so, their attitude conveying mute respect. Spinoza took the offered hand and shook it, matching ounce for ounce the pressure in that grip. He kept his face impassive.

"I'm Frank Spinoza. Welcome to Las Vegas."

"Jake Pinelli. Glad that we could help you out. No problem with the rooms?"

"My house is yours."

"Okay. Just let us settle in, and we can all get down to business."

"Good."

A movement on his flank distracted him, and Spinoza saw a runner huddling with Paulie, speaking to him in a whisper. Paulie heard him out, dismissed him, and then, before Spinoza could direct the New York crew chief to his suite, the houseman cleared his throat, discreetly claiming Frank's attention.

"Say, Frank...."

"Hang on a minute, Paulie. Now—"

"You got a call, boss. On your private line. It sounds important."

"Dammit, Paulie—"

"Never mind," Pinelli interjected, frowning. "We'll find our way. Go take your call."

"I'll have some food sent up. You name it, Jake."

"We caught some dinner on the plane, but thanks. I'll just wait till you get your action squared away."

Spinoza, fuming, followed Paulie back in the direction of his private office. He would have to watch Pinelli closely, make damn sure the snotty bastard did not start to think he was in charge. Too many chiefs were bad for business, and Spinoza meant to be the only honcho at the Gold Rush.

Hell, he meant to be the only honcho in Las Vegas.

Alone inside his office he relaxed a fraction, slumping down into his high-backed chair and punching up the lighted button for his private number as he lifted the receiver to his ear.

"Yeah?"

Momentary silence on the other end, finally broken by a voice that was distinctly male, distinctly cautious.

"I needta speak to Mr. Frank Spinoza."

There was a trace of Eastern Seaboard in the voice, which he could not identify with any more precision.

"You got him."

"Yeah? I mean, good evening, sir."

"Who am I talking to?"

"Just call me Joe from Jersey. I'm connected back there with the Drucci family."

Sure, it fit. The Jersey twang.

Spinoza was not taking any chances with the caller being who he claimed to be.

"I've got some friends in Jersey," he allowed. "How's old Vinnie Giacovelli doing these days?"

Hesitation, but the caller caught on fast.

"He died six months ago. You ought to know that, sir."

"Okay. So, Joe from Jersey, how'd you get this number?"

"I guess you'd say it was a backup, sir. A kinda last resort...just covering all the bases, like, you know?"

"Somebody said this was important."

"Well...yeah, it might be. Anyhow, I thought I'd better tip you when I heard about your troubles."

"Troubles?" Spinoza was hard pressed to hide his irritation.

"Uh, yeah. That's kinda why I called. I thought you oughta know...about what I heard."

Spinoza kept his tone civil now with an effort.

"I guess I don't follow you, Joe."

"Well, I picked up a broad downtown this evening—what a looker, man, the jugs on this one—anyway, we stopped into this restaurant she likes. A Japanese place. Me, I don't care much for all that seafood shit, but hell...whatever turns 'em on, you know? I mean—"

Spinoza interrupted him. "Where is this place?"

"On Paradise. It had some kinda flowers in the name."

"The Lotus Garden."

It was not a question.

"Yeah, that's it. Well, anyhow—where was I?"

"In the restaurant."

"Oh, yeah. So we're just sitting there and this babe's sucking up the fish, but me, I'm concentrating on dessert, when I make out these two Nips talking shop behind me in another booth."

"Go on."

"I wouldn'a paid attention in the first place, but I heard some names that rang a bell, you know. These gooks were naming you, Liguori, Johnny Cats—some others I don't know for sure."

"What did they say?"

"Well, that's just it, sir. They were switching in and out with Japanese and some damn kinda broken English, so I couldn't get too much, but...."

"Anything at all, Joe." Spinoza's voice was cold as ice now, almost brittle.

"Right, okay. One guy says something like, 'The troops are in,' and then they go back into Japanese a while. But I can still make out your name, the Gold Rush, this and that."

"Go on."

"Well, they go back and forth like that and most of it is all this gook palaver, but then one of them comes out and says, 'Tonight. We go tonight,' like that. I mean, it doesn't take no Einstein now to figure out they're running down a hit on your place for this evening.''

"And that's all of it?"

"It's all that I could understand. They took off pretty quick, and I hauled ass myself. I figured you should hear about this right away.''

"You did the right thing, Joe. I wanna thank you.''

"Hey, we're all *amici*, right? I could stop by . . . I mean, I've got a piece if you could use an extra hand.''

"I think we've got it covered here, but thanks again. I'll thank your capo personally when I get the chance.''

"Hell, that ain't necessary, sir.''

"I think it is.''

"Well . . . thank you.''

"If you ever feel the urge to relocate out east—you know, to get some sun . . . .''

"I might at that.''

"Okay, Joe. Have a safe trip home.''

"And you, sir. Don't take any shit offa those Nips.''

"Good night, Joe.''

Frank Spinoza put the phone down gently. His mind was racing into confrontation with the danger that awaited him outside in the darkness of the desert night.

Somehow Kuwahara had found out about his buildup at the Gold Rush, and he had been working on a countermove—his own preemptive strike.

Well, two could play that little game. Spinoza had the troops on hand to end this thing in one decisive move.

It was time for Jake Pinelli and his guns to earn their money. He would send Paulie with them, just to be sure they did it right the first time and to see that all his interests were protected.

When they finished mopping up the streets with Kuwahara's chopsticks . . . well, Spinoza meant to have a little send-off waiting for them at the Gold Rush. A going-away that none of them would soon forget. For the survivors.

As for the rest...there was a great big desert out there waiting to be filled with little graves, and Frank Spinoza had a corner on the shovel market. He was going to get a lot of digging done before the bloody sunrise came up over Vegas one more time.

And it would not be Kuwahara's rising run. No way. *His* sun was going down in flames, except the Jap was too damned dumb to know it yet.

The sun was rising for Spinoza and his family. The Nevada family. And they were going to flourish in the light.

MACK BOLAN—LATELY KNOWN as Joe from Jersey— eased the telephone receiver down and lit himself a cigarette. He was anticipating the results of his brief conversation with Spinoza, what the aftershock would mean for Seiji Kuwahara, for the Mafia...and for the city of Las Vegas.

He had cruised by the Gold Rush earlier, observed the hard-eyed types unloading from their chauffeured limos, mobbing up at the hotel–casino. They were going hard down there, about to put an army on the streets, and from his knowledge of the Mafia mind, Bolan knew that when the killing started they would not be taking time to sift out innocent civilians from the line of fire.

West was ready to collide with East and countless lives were hanging in the balance. All of Vegas could become a battleground—unless the Executioner's device turned out to be successful.

He had called Spinoza in the hope of giving him a target, drawing off the savages from roving street patrol and pitting them against the common enemy where they would do least damage to the innocents around them. Kuwahara's hardsite seemed the perfect place to bring them all together. Any troops who hung back at the Gold Rush, left on garrison duty with Spinoza, would be waiting for him when he finished with the spearhead.

He dropped another dime and dialed the number of a giant Strip hotel, his eyes upon the traffic sliding past his phone booth while the operator put him through to Tommy Anders's room. The comic's voice was cautious as he answered.

"Yes?"

"How is she?"

Hesitation on the other end.

"Well. . .ah, dammit, man, she split."

And something cold turned over in the soldier's stomach.

"What happened, Joker?"

"I was only in the next room for a minute, maybe two, just touching base with Wonderland. When I came back there was no sign of her."

"How long?"

"I'd say an hour, maybe less."

The warrior's mind ran through some alternate scenarios, but none of them provided him the slightest reassurance. Finally, reluctantly, he put the woman out of mind and went ahead with business.

"Let me have another hour, Joker, then put through a call to Metro Homicide. The man you want is Captain Reese."

"Okay. I've got it."

"Tell him that Spinoza has a crew at Seiji Kuwahara's, and they're bringing down the house. He'll know the address."

"Kuwahara's, right. Hey, Sarge. . . ."

"Forget it."

"Can't. I'm sorry that I let her get away."

"She wasn't ours to hold," the warrior told him. And again, "Forget about it."

But the soldier would have trouble following his own advice that night. Lucy Bernstein was in danger, right, and there was nothing either he or Tommy Anders could have done to keep her safe and sound.

The choice was hers, and she had made it freely. And he understood why. She had a job to do and she had gone about it on her own.

She was a big girl. He only hoped she had the sense to find herself a shelter from the rising storm that was about to sweep the city.

There was no way he could stop the wheels that had been set in motion here tonight.

The Universe was in the driver's seat and all of them were booked through to the end of the line, wherever, whatever that end turned out to be.

For some, perhaps for all of them, the vehicle would prove to be a hearse—but none of them could disembark before they reached the final destination preordained by fate.

The Executioner stubbed out his smoke and left the phone booth, moving through the darkness toward his waiting rental car. He had no wish to put off the inevitable; on the contrary, he welcomed the future whatever it might bring.

For he had done his duty, and he would continue doing it while life and strength remained. Tonight, tomorrow—for as long as he was given, he would fight the good fight, carry on and spread his cleansing fire among the dark encampments of the universal enemy.

The Executioner was moving toward a rendezvous with destiny in the desert, with a stopover in hell along the way.

19

Paradise Valley lies south of Las Vegas and east of the Strip. It has been colonized by well-to-do casino personnel and such show-business stars as chose to live in Vegas through the off months, when they are not on the road. A spacious area with mammoth homes and ready access to four separate country clubs, the neighborhood enjoys a reputation for conspicuous consumption, and the residents take pride in their affluence.

In the fifties they elected old Gus Greenbaum mayor of Paradise, deciding that his quasi-ownership of the flamboyant Riviera Hotel and Casino necessarily outfitted him for public office. Everyone professed surprise when Gus, a one-time murderer and closet junkie, ran afoul of mafiosi who were really putting strings down at the Riviera.

He was on vacation at the family home in Arizona when somebody hacked his head off with a butcher knife and then went on to practice further surgical techniques upon Mrs. Greenbaum in the next room, taking time to spread out plastic tarps beneath each body prior to cutting.

And the folks back home in Paradise could well appreciate the hit team's grim fastidiousness. No maid could ever clean those twenty pints of blood out of a Persian carpet.

And Paradise had made almost a cult of looking clean, of putting up appearances and hiding in the shadows. Driving down the tree-lined streets and looking at palatial homes in back of finely manicured lawns, no casual tourist would suspect which houses had been built with skimmed casino money, cash from tax frauds and insurance swindles.

If your next-door neighbor was in league with mobsters, if he was a practicing arsonist who torched his own concerns for profit, well...the world was dog-eat-dog, and every businessman had overhead to meet. As long as you could settle out of court with IRS or dodge the audits altogether, there was no real reason for concern.

And if you took the fall there would be someone waiting for the house, with ready cash in hand.

Someone like Seiji Kuwahara, the businessman from Tokyo who specialized in restaurants—and other things. His neighbors knew him vaguely, did not seek acquaintance with him on a daily basis, but if asked, they would assure investigators that there could be nothing wrong with Mr. Kuwahara. How could any criminal keep such nice flower gardens, after all?

Mack Bolan smelled the flowers—and the stench of death that drowned their sweet fragrance like the reek of fresh-laid fertilizer. Crouching in the darkness, sweeping Seiji Kuwahara's desert palace with his night eyes, the Executioner knew that he was looking at a dragon's lair.

The residential neighborhood had not been Bolan's first choice for a battlefield, but it was preferable to the Lotus Garden, down on Paradise, where stray fire might encounter any one of several hundred tourists still abroad and seeking action. Here, at least, the residents were either still out for the evening, or else settled safely in behind their triple locks and burglar bars.

It was the best that he could do, right, and the place would simply have to serve his purposes.

He had come dressed for combat, decked out in the nightsuit that clung to him like a second skin, its hidden pockets filled with slim stiletto, strangling gear, the grim accoutrements of silent death.

The silenced Beretta 93-R hung beneath his left arm in its shoulder harness, and Big Thunder, the .44 AutoMag, occupied its usual place on his right hip, hung on military webbing. Nylon pouches circling his waist held extra magazines for both the handguns, prearranged to let him find them by their feel alone amid the smoke and dust of battle.

Slung across his back was a Mini-Uzi submachine gun, fully loaded. Inches shorter than its parent weapon, the little stuttergun had not surrendered any of its man-breaking firepower when it was miniaturized. Roughly the size of an Ingram MAC-10 with its side-folding stock, the little Uzi could lay down its parabellum manglers at a cyclic rate of 1,200 rounds per minute—a cataclysmic outpouring that Bolan had himself refined to a more manageable 750 rpm.

Head weapon for the evening was a recent Bolan favorite, the XM-18 semiautomatic projectile launcher. Built on the revolver principle, the XM-18 sported a 12-shot rotary magazine.

Constructed out of coated steel and durable cast aluminum to cut the weight, it was a one-man piece of field artillery, and Bolan could unload its twelve big chambers in the space of half as many seconds when the heat was on. The rifled bore belonging to the 40mm model made hits possible out to the weapon's maximum effective range of 150 yards, and with a steady hand, the cannon could work miracles against the opposition.

Double belts of premixed rounds encircled Bolan's chest, combining high-explosive rounds with gas and smoke, fléchette and shot—enough to give an army pause, damn right.

Which was exactly what the soldier meant to do.

Fifteen minutes had passed since Bolan spoke with

Tommy Anders, and the mental clock was ticking off the numbers. The pace was picking up now, the Las Vegas caldron coming to a boil around him. Precision timing was the key if Bolan did not mean to wind up as a piece of well-done meat left floating in the stew pot.

He was counting on Spinoza to dispatch an army straight for Kuwahara's, armed for war. The mafioso might be having trouble with his men, collecting all the arms he needed for the raid . . . but even so they should be on the scene at any moment now.

Inside the walls he could pick out a moving human figure here and there, primarily keeping to the shadows and avoiding the noonday glare of strategically positioned floodlights. It was far too late for gardeners, and from the glimpse that Bolan got on one occasion as his target inadvertently stepped into light, the slender men in tailored business suits had never done a day of spadework in their lives.

Unless, perhaps, they had been planting bodies in the desert lately.

Bolan counted half a dozen of them behind the low retaining wall, and knew there would be more where those came from. A man like Kuwahara, taking on the Mafia by choice, would not sleep well at night without an army at his beck and call. The question for Mack Bolan now revolved around how many men were in there, and how many guns they had at their disposal. He had come prepared to buck the odds, and yet—

A stab of light in his peripheral vision claimed the Executioner's attention. He half turned, just in time to see the tag end of a four-car caravan as it negotiated the right-hand turn and fell back into line with the procession rolling down the avenue toward Kuwahara's mansion. Four black Lincolns, six-door models with jump seats down that would accommodate from twenty-four to thirty gunners, depending on how tightly they were packed in there.

An army, right.

And from the way they cut their lights a half block down, approaching like a ghostly funeral cortege with only street lamps left to guide them on, they had not come in peace.

A pair of Kuwahara's men materialized from out of nowhere just inside the decorative wrought-iron gates. They were watching as the line of limousines approached now, reaching underneath their tailored jackets, coming out again with hardware. Bolan used the opportunity to take the low retaining wall in one smooth motion, landing in a combat crouch among the occupant's prize-winning roses.

He moved away from there, preferring empty shadows and the smell of new-mown grass to the funeral-parlor perfume of the flower garden.

He was settling into other cover, downrange, when the leader of the limo caravan decided he had had enough of caution. Standing on his Lincoln's accelerator, the wheelman cut hard left and brought his tank squealing up the short driveway from street to gates, rear tires smoking as they ate the pavement.

Kuwahara's guards each fired a futile round or two in the direction of the juggernaut, then leaped away to either side as the Detroit torpedo met the gates, plowing on through to the accompaniment of grinding, screeching steel.

A clap of gunfire drowned the sound of falling numbers in his head, and Bolan moved out, traveling on instinct now. From here on in, reconnaissance was next to worthless, planning almost pointless. There were too damn many wild cards in the game, and any combination of them came out to the dead man's hand.

The soldier took a firm grip on the XM-18, leaving cover in a rush. He knew only one strategy for playing when the stakes were life and death. You bet the limit.

INSIDE HIS PRIVATE STUDY Seiji Kuwahara contemplated strategy in silence, eyes and mind closed to the world around him. A casual observer might have thought he was asleep, and any passing medical examiner would certainly have given him a second glance for vital signs, but Kuwahara was in fact both conscious and alert. And he had problems.

He was concerned by the reports of military buildups at the Gold Rush, gunners flying in from eastward, others already in town, arriving by the carload. Somehow, something had occurred that forced the disparate Mafia factions to seek their safety in numbers, cooperating for the moment where they normally were barely speaking.

It might have been the raid on Bob Minotte, but the man from Tokyo was not convinced. Minotte was not popular among his fellow capos, and as long as the entire threat seemed to be directed at his camp, it seemed unlikely that the others would do more than pay lip service to their high ideals of brotherhood.

Still there were reports of violence at the Gold Rush earlier that afternoon. His man inside Spinoza's camp had been unable to provide in-depth reports, but there appeared to have been some shooting, even loss of life.

Kuwahara was worried that something might be about to spoil his master plan. He had intended to divide and conquer, take the mafiosi piecemeal, but now they seemed to be presenting him with a united front.

That meant a sudden change in strategy but he was equal to the challenge. A simple shift of gears and he could easily accommodate the new requirements of the war that he had chosen to initiate.

It might be helpful, after all, to have his enemies collected at the Gold Rush. Narrow down the targets...concentrate your fire. And yet, his group was not large enough to risk a full-out frontal raid against a force that seemed to number in the vicinity of sixty guns. There would be more by now, for sure, with locals coming in to bolster up the ranks. And while he had faith in his little clique of samurai, he did not wish to waste them when the odds were four or five to one.

Seiji Kuwahara was a tactician not a betting man.

If there was some way he could infiltrate a *ninja* team into the Gold Rush, have them seek out and annihilate the capos assembled there...ah, it would have made his life so much less complicated. Another suicide mission, of course. But then, his troops were brought up in the way of the samurai, preferring death to failure and dishonor.

He would think about the infiltration process, but in the meantime there was the matter of simple personal defense to be considered. Frank Spinoza and the others would be coming for him, one way or another—at the restaurant, at some public appearance, anywhere—and Kuwahara knew he must be ready for them.

The time was past for him to place some calls...to San Francisco and Los Angeles, for starters. He needed reinforcements now, and if he made the calls this evening troops could be at his disposal by tomorrow.

The first faint sounds of gunfire reached his ears like pinpricks stabbing at his psyche, piercing through the veil of meditation, opening his senses to the outside stimulus. And close behind he heard the grinding shriek of steel on steel.

Before he knew it, Kuwahara's heart was in his throat, leaving him alone with only raw emotion for a shield. He was too late. The calls he contemplated could not bring him help in time. He was trapped.

Not yet.

The man from Tokyo regained a measure of his inner strength, reminding himself that an assault upon his house was not a victory his enemies could celebrate unless they reached him, killed or captured him. He could elude them still, perhaps defeat them with the force he kept on hand for such emergencies.

There would be time enough to place those calls an hour from now, he reasoned. Time enough to carry out a new offensive.

His house was under siege by savages, and when the man from Tokyo had dealt with them, there would be more than ample time to ponder suitable reprisals on their masters.

Kuwahara left his study, moving with renewed determination toward the battlefront. His troops had need of him, and he of them. Together they were strong, and in their strength lay victory.

MOVING THROUGH THE DARKNESS in a combat crouch, Bolan counted off the limos as they cleared the gate. The first was through and running clear, the windows down. Automatic weapons were spitting jagged tongues of flame in all directions at the gunners who were bold or foolhardy enough to show themselves. Behind it, numbers two and three broke through in tandem, rattling right across the twisted remains of Seiji Kuwahara's decorative gates.

He waited until number four was nosing through, then he raised the XM-18. Sighting quickly down the stubby barrel he stroked off a high-explosive round and rode out the negligible recoil, watching as his can impacted on the Lincoln's nose. There was a flash, a crack of heavy-metal thunder ripping through the night, and the crew wagon lurched to an abrupt halt, shattered engine dying in an instant.

Doors were springing open down there, the surviving occupants unwilling to sit still and wait for flames or the incoming rounds to seek them out like sitting ducks.

The warrior left them to it, satisfied that he had plugged the only exit, moving on in search of other targets in the hellgrounds.

All around him small-arms fire was rippling through the night, most of it concentrating on the three remaining Lincolns as they powered along the curving drive toward Kuwahara's mansion. The other drivers either had not missed their tail car, or else they had decided that the crewmen were expendable.

And Bolan tipped his hat to savage loyalty, knowing that the cannibals would turn upon their own to save themselves. It was a trait that had assisted him before in time of need, and might again.

He paced the Lincolns, tracking them on foot and keeping to the far left of the driveway, letting those cars draw the full attention and the hostile fire of Kuwahara's soldiers. They were taking hits out there, but armored bodywork and bullet-proof glass would keep the gunners safe until they ventured out and into range.

The Executioner had no such shield around him, and he welcomed the diversion that Spinoza's spearhead was providing for him as he made his way across the darkened lawn.

Another fifty yards of grass and asphalt separated Bolan from the house when Frank Spinoza's hit team reached their destination. There was no way to continue with their strike except on foot. Reluctantly they started bailing out of the protection offered by the limousines, lithe figures darting underneath the floodlights, laying down a furious covering fire, some of the more adventurous souls advancing on the house.

Mack Bolan hit a crouch and swung his launcher up, not needing pinpoint accuracy now that he was this close to the target. He stroked the trigger once, already pivoting and firing off round two before his first can found its target and erupted into roiling flames.

In front of him another Continental reared up on its haunches, riding the crest of a firewave, and settled slowly back down to burning earth. The men who had been crouching behind it were sent scattering in panic. Several of them were sprawled out beneath the shock wave, slapping at the flames that blossomed in their hair and clothing.

Target number two was Seiji Kuwahara's house itself, and Bolan watched the high-explosive round as it impacted on the double doors in front, the hand-carved panels seeming to implode then disappear within a cloud of smoke and plaster dust. A strangled scream came from somewhere inside, and the responding automatic fire was momentarily silenced as surviving gunners scrambled to seek out new vantage points.

Along the fashionable drive, the lights were coming on in other houses as residents were roused from sleep or sluggish dinner-party conversation, forced to notice what was going on outside their own protective walls.

The Devil was in Paradise, for damn sure, dwelling in the dragon's lair, and he was fighting for his life against a new St. George decked out in blackface and a suit of midnight fabric. It was mortal combat within easy access of the country club, and neither side would leave the field so long as life and strength remained.

It would be Hell in Paradise this night, a firestorm blowing through the placid streets, invading apathetic lives and spewing shrapnel through their curtains of complacency.

The Executioner was here and he was blitzing on.

20

Seiji Kuwahara reached the bottom of the curving staircase just in time to watch his marbled entryway explode, the double doors collapsing inward with a thunderclap. There was fire, he saw that much, and then the man from Tokyo was clearing the stairs in a rush and seeking sanctuary toward the rear of the house.

Somehow, Spinoza's men had come upon him unaware, and now they were upon his doorstep, pouring automatic fire into his very home. The Yakuza ambassador was not quite sure how such a thing had come about, but he would have to shoulder the responsibility in any case. The failure, any shame attached to it, was his.

He knew that any one of his superiors in Tokyo would face disaster of this sort with equanimity that was predictable and loathsome. Staring at defeat they would find refuge in seppuku, the ancient time-honored escape hatch of suicide. And they would expect the same, no doubt, from Kuwahara in his present situation.

But Seiji meant to disappoint them on that score.

His studies of the West and of the Mafia had taught him many things—not least of which had been the sheer futility of killing oneself whenever things looked dark. He learned that those who won success in America were those who hung on through adversity, who never gave an inch, but rather kept on fighting toward the dream they cherished.

In the end their perseverance and tenacity were what made them winners.

And Seiji Kuwahara meant to be a winner.

Even now, with hot flames licking at his back and automatic weapons streaming fire into the foyer of his one-time palatial home, he knew that he could salvage something from the situation if he kept his wits about him. Even if Spinoza's soldiers overran his house, there would be other times and other chances to exact his retribution.

If he lived.

Exactly.

And his first priority was getting out of there, removing himself from the scene of the action and finding a safe place where he could bide his time, regroup his forces, mount another campaign against the Mafia Brotherhood.

He was reminded, strangely, of a game that he had played in childhood with his brothers. Each of them would raise a fist, and on the count of three an open hand would be displayed in one of three configurations. Two extended fingers were the scissors; a flat hand was the paper; and a closed fist was the stone.

Seiji could still remember the childish litany as if it had been only yesterday. *Scissors cut paper, paper wraps stone, stone blunts scissors.*

He was the stone to Frank Spinoza's scissors, yes, and if he did not blunt them here, with force, then he could change his shape and become the paper that would wrap and smother the mafioso's stone.

His victory was preordained, Kuwahara thought. It was his karma to achieve preeminence in his chosen field, and anything that happened in the here and now was mere digression.

He met the first contingent of his *ninja* in the corridor that led to the kitchen. They were on their way to battle, armed and ready. He stopped them and issued other orders in the curt clipped tones of his beloved native tongue. They understood and would not dare question anything he said, no matter how bizarre they might consider his orders to be. They would do anything he asked, short of dishonoring themselves, and they would see him now to safety if that was his wish.

It was.

The little human caravan doubled back through the kitchen and toward the rear of the big house where Kuwahara's limousine was stowed in the garage. There was no firing yet from that direction and the man from Tokyo was hoping he could get a jump on anyone who might be trying to outflank him by attacking from the rear.

They would still have to run the gauntlet of the driveway, certainly, but anything was preferable to sitting here, waiting for the roof to fall around his ears.

Another loud explosion rocked the house and Kuwahara cringed involuntarily. The place had cost him better than a million dollars to construct but it was only money. Seiji had lives to save. One very near and dear life in particular.

He let the *ninja* lead him out of there, his eyes and mind already set upon another brighter day, when he would see the rising sun above Las Vegas like a battle flag of old Nippon. That day was coming soon and when it came, he would be well and whole to lead the troops—his troops—to victory against Spinoza and the rest. The stars had told him so.

HE HAD BEEN HALF EXPECTING the call, and when the black phone on his desk began to ring, Sam Reese sat glaring at it for a moment before answering. He knew that any news arriving this late would be bad news and he braced himself for the worst.

He was not disappointed.

The caller reported shooting, out at Seiji Kuwahara's

place in Paradise. They said it sounded like a goddamn war was going on out there—and Reese had no doubt they were probably correct.

He cursed and cradled the receiver with more force than necessary. There had been a time when Paradise Valley was out of his jurisdiction, back before the Clark County Sheriff's Office had merged with metro. But now the shooting war at Kuwahara's had been placed directly in his lap. The homicide detective had to deal with it while he had a chance to end the carnage with a swift decisive stroke.

LaMancha's words came back to him like haunting prophecy, and Reese cursed again as he snared his jacket en route to the door.

He wondered where the big Fed was, and what he had to do with this, if anything. Most likely he was shacked up in a plush hotel suite somewhere, riding out the storm and taking time between his cocktails to type up a fine report about the inefficiency of Metro's tactical response.

Well, screw him. Reese was rolling now, and there were SWAT teams on the way already. Every black-and-white within a five-mile radius was on its way to Kuwahara's with sirens screaming. In another couple of minutes, the joint would look like a goddamned metro convention, and Reese planned to kick some ass when he got there.

It would be terrible if Kuwahara and Spinoza should get caught in the cross fire and both end up in drawers down at the county morgue. Too much to hope for, and yet....

This might just be the end of Seiji Kuwahara's plans in Vegas. Some good might come from this, some chance for Sam Reese and his town to settle back to normal.

He put the thought out of his mind, concentrating on

the grim reality of the present situation. He was about to step into a killing zone, something he had not faced since Korea, and he knew that he would need full concentration to see him through the coming hours.

And where was Mack Bolan when you needed him?

The question came up out of nowhere, circled several times around the homicide captain's subconscious before it broke the surface like a cruising dorsal fin. As quickly as it formed, he put the thought out of mind, a little shudder racing down his spine.

That was the last thing he needed now, damn right. Another wild man in the streets when he already had two frigging armies at each other's throats. The very last thing in the world.

And still. . . .

He hit the double doors to the garage, already calling out to the stray uniforms who were standing around waiting to begin or end their shifts. They would be going with him, filling in the ranks for what looked like the biggest sit-down bloodfeast in Las Vegas history. And there would be enough to go around for everybody, he was sure, perhaps with seconds for the hungry ones.

Goddammit, and the thought was back, refusing just to die and blow away like desert sand.

Where was Mack Bolan when you needed him?

PAULIE VACCARELLI snapped a wild shot in the general direction of the house and ducked back under cover, wincing as a stray round glanced off fender metal inches from his head. The previous explosion, caused by God-knew-what, had calmed them down in there for something like a half a minute, but the bastards had regrouped, and they were pouring out defensive fire again as if they had a million rounds to spare.

And maybe they did, Paulie thought, the grim notion

ricocheting back and forth inside his mind until he got a grip on it and put it down where it belonged.

No million rounds, no way. His troop had taken Kuwahara's people by surprise, and they were fighting back the way Japs always fought—with everything they had. But they were losing, right, surrounded by some of the toughest gunners he had ever seen, cut off from any possible escape.

Cut off.

He risked a backward glance in the direction of the gates, and saw the Lincoln was still burning brightly, all four tires melted down, the limo resting on its belly in the middle of the driveway like a flaming dinosaur carcass.

Paulie wondered what the hell had happened to it, just exploding like that. Maybe some kind of land mine, or some other kind of goddamn booby trap—except, why had the Japs let three cars through, then blown up the last one.

Why?

To trap your ass, you stupid jerk.

He shrugged, refusing to acknowledge the idea that they had suckered him somehow, prepared a trap that would be inescapable.

One of the gate guards just got lucky, maybe with some kind of armor-piercing round, or maybe even with one of those frigging grenade launchers you were always hearing about. No telling what kind of hardware that goddamn Kuwahara had floating around, with his contacts in Tokyo and Vietnam or wherever.

Paulie risked a glance above the Lincoln's hood and almost lost it as another automatic burst came sizzling in from the direction of the house. The bullets hit the armored bodywork and whined away, but he still felt terribly exposed out there, despite the bulwark of the lii that protected him from any head-on fire.

Beside him, Jake Pinelli was chafing at the bit, anxious to get in there and start wasting Kuwahara's troops. He jabbed at Paulie with the muzzle of his silenced Ingram, leaning forward and raising his voice to make himself heard above the din of battle.

"We've gotta get in there, goddammit! We can't just sit around out here all night and wait for the cops to come in on our blind side."

The cops.

Paulie had forgotten them when all the shit had started flying, but he knew Pinelli was correct. It could not be long now before the first patrol cars made the scene, and he for one did not intend to face a lineup charged with multiple counts of homicide. Not for the sake of some yellow bastard like Seiji Kuwahara.

"Okay," he snapped back, reluctant in spite of the new urgency he felt. "Let's take 'em."

"Right."

And Jake Pinelli was already rising from his crouch with a long burst from the Ingram, raking the front of Kuwahara's house as he charged out of cover and into the direct line of fire.

Paulie watched him, frozen where he sat, his hand white knuckled where it gripped the walnut stock of his .357. He could not force himself to take the necessary first step, could not make himself get up and follow Jake Pinelli through the hellgrounds.

And the New York gunner made it maybe twenty feet before converging fire ripped into him and through him, spraying crimson back along his track so that huge globs of him spattered on the Lincoln's bullet-scarred hood ⸻ Paulie felt something wet sting his face and ⸻ of sight, vainly willing his mind to erase ⸻ at he had seen. Of what might have been ⸻

⸻ apped, he acknowledged it now, and if

Kuwahara's samurai could not find an exit, neither could the troops who still survived outside the house. He tried a hasty head count, stopping short of two full carloads when another bullet snapped the smoky air beside his ear.

They had lost something like half of their force already with no end in sight, and Paulie Vaccarelli started concentrating on a way to disengage the enemy without losing the other half in a blind-assed retreat. The point, after all, was to get out alive, and he would worry about Spinoza and the consequences of his failure when he was safe on the other side of that frigging wall two hundred yards distant.

He froze, staring at it through the smoky night.

The wall.

If he could make it—

Paulie stopped dead in his tracks before he could translate the thought to action. There were others here who were his responsibility. He could not run and leave them here to make it on their own. They were depending on him. And yet—

His thoughts were swallowed by the sound of another explosion, and Paulie turned back toward the sound just in time to see an upstairs-window casing shiver and disintegrate, expelling bits of wood and plaster with a flaming body, everything raining down on the steps twenty feet in front of his position.

He scanned the battlefield, taking advantage of a momentary lull in the cross fire to check out his surroundings. Suddenly he saw a nightmare figure moving toward him through the battle murk.

The man was tall and muscular, clad in something like a black skinsuit, carrying the largest tommy gun Paulie had ever seen. The guy's face was black—but whether he was made up or a natural, Paulie could not say. His full attention now was centered on the smoking weapon that the big guy carried, and he knew instinctively that he was looking at the source of the explosions that had ripped the night apart.

Whatever else he was, the guy was no damned Japanese, but Paulie had to figure that he was responsible for taking out the two demolished Lincolns. If he had also blasted Kuwahara's house, then that was fine. But clearly this one was not taking sides. Instead he seemed intent on wiping both sides out, and that was where Paul Vaccarelli drew the frigging line.

Spinoza's hardman lurched erect, his big .357 Magnum out in front of him and steadied in both hands, the sights wavering briefly before they came to rest on the big guy's chest. He was an easy target, right, if only Paulie could make his goddamned hands stop shaking so much.

Downrange, the big man seemed to sense his danger, pivoting in the direction of Paulie's position, the ash-can muzzle of his weapon tracking with him, belching flame before poor Paulie could notice a finger on the cannon's trigger. The high-explosive can impacted on the Lincoln's nose, punching on through the grille to detonate beneath the hood with thunderous effect.

Vaccarelli was driven backward, sprawling on the grass, his Magnum flying. Miraculously, he made it to his feet, coming out of the somersault erect, ears ringing from the near concussion of the blast. He glanced around, but there was something warm and sticky in his eyes, and he was being blinded by the smoke from—

Holy mother, from his own damned jacket burning! Paulie Vaccarelli knew that he was standing there on fire, and then the panic hit him, made him run, the black-clad stranger long forgotten as he streaked across the night, a racing human torch.

THE BURNING SCARECROW FIGURE lurched along for half a dozen strides, then Bolan saw it toppled by a rifle shot. Inside the house the gunners were attempting to regroup their forces, and the flaming silhouette had been a target too inviting to resist.

He swung their way and sent a high-explosive double-punch through the ruin of the twin front doors, following it up with a hissing can of smoke to add confusion. The house was burning fiercely now at several points, and Bolan knew that there were only moments left until he heard the wail of sirens on his flank, announcing the approach of riot squads responding to the din and smoke of combat.

It was a roaring hell in there, but Bolan had to get inside and seek out Seiji Kuwahara, close down this end of the pipeline before the Executioner took another step along the campaign trail in Vegas. He knew from grim experience in the jungles of the world that you exposed yourself to needless danger any time you left the serpent's head intact, still able to deliver lethal venom even with its dying spasm.

Kuwahara was the Oriental viper's head in Vegas, and when Bolan had disposed of this one, there were others of an Occidental cast who called for his attention, right. But first things first.

He was advancing on the house, prepared to answer fire with cleansing fire when Bolan heard a labored engine drawing closer on his flank. Almost before the sound had registered, a sleek white Caddy cleared the side of Kuwahara's mansion, running straight and fast along an offshoot of the drive and making for the gates.

There was just time for Bolan to react, half turning, catching just the barest glimpse of Eastern profile, then the limousine was past him, powering along the drive.

The soldier hit a crouch and braced the 40mm cannon tight against his hip, one finger on the trigger as he tracked his target, estimating range and elevation.

When he opened fire, the Executioner was dead on target at a range of fifty yards, the mushrooming explosions marching right across the driveway, setting up a barrier of smoke and flying shrapnel that the hurtling Caddy could not bridge. He saw the crew wagon swerve, lurch, stall, and he was moving out of there and into confrontation with the dragon long before the first door opened, spilling human targets into view.

Mack Bolan recognized the *ninja* at a range of thirty yards, and spent no time debating how to handle him. The XM-18 thundered and the guy was simply gone, evaporated in a storm of needlelike fléchettes that hit with such intensity he doubtless never knew that he was dying.

And they were packed inside the Cadillac, the *ninja* trying to get out and face the enemy, a little man wedged in among them with his hands raised, trying desperately to shield himself from the death he saw approaching.

Bolan knew that he had found the serpent's head. A twitch of his trigger finger and the launcher roared to life, unloading its remaining cylinders in rapid fire; fléchettes, shot and high-explosives all impacting on the Cadillac's interior like a draft from hell itself.

The windows on the Caddy blew outward and the crew wagon seemed to bulge for a moment, inflating like some kind of cartoon vehicle before it simply burst apart. Bolan rode out the shock wave and went to ground beneath the flying shrapnel, feeling pieces of the vehicle and occupants as they rained down around him in a grizzly downpour.

And from the distance, drawing nearer—sirens.

He could hear the numbers falling in his mind, their echoes louder than the straggling gunfire that continued from inside the Kuwahara house. Some of the enemy were still engaged back there, but he no longer had an interest in them. Captain Reese and his commandos would be more than capable of dealing with the stragglers. And Bolan had more serpents left to kill this night before the desert sun came up and burned away the sheltering darkness.

He was far from finished in Las Vegas, right.

If anything the major battle lay ahead, and he had only fought a skirmish here with Kuwahara's men and the advance guard from New York.

If he had severed and destroyed one viper's head, the whole damned nest awaited him downtown, and he did not intend to keep the serpents waiting long. The Executioner was done in Paradise, the snakes were driven out—for now—and he was moving on.

To Glitter Gulch.

To the Gold Rush.

To Frank Spinoza and the good-old boys.

If they were waiting for him now...for *some-one*—braced for trouble—then there would be killing in the Mafia's open city such as Captain Reese had never seen.

21

"All right, we're set to go."

Abe Bernstein looked around him at the faces of his soldiers. Then his eyes fell on Jack Goldblume and old Harry Thorson, feeling pride well up inside of him until he was about to burst. It took a moment for him to continue but he finally found his voice.

"Spinoza's men have run into some kinda trouble at Kuwahara's and they won't be back. At least not soon. We've got a chance to clean it up tonight if everybody does his job and follows orders."

He turned to the tall mercenary dressed in a hotel security uniform, raising one eyebrow as he spoke.

"Your people in position?"

"Yes, sir. This hotel is sealed off tight. Nobody in or out without your say-so."

"Fine." The old man nodded satisfaction. "All of you have team assignments, wings to cover. . . . Are there any problems?"

"Hell, no," Harry Thorson growled around the stub of his cigar. "Let's quit the goddamn jawin' and get on with it."

Bernstein smiled, half turning toward Goldblume.

"Square with you, Jack?"

"Fine."

But there was something in the newsman's voice that made Bernstein uneasy. A trace of weakness, perhaps. The taint of fear.

He had arranged for two of Goldblume's team to

watch him through the night, dispose of him if he seemed likely to jeopardize the mission. Their friendship spanned four decades, but tonight Abe Bernstein was about to realize a lifelong dream. And no damned friend was going to cheat him out of it, no way. If Goldblume pulled his weight fine, but if he tried to weasel out . . . .

Bernstein dismissed the topic from his mind and checked his Rolex.

"Okay. We start on top and work our way down, clearing each floor as we go, and meet back here within the hour. Cleanup detail starts at 1:00 A.M. What do you military fellows call it?"

"Oh-one-hundred hours," the tall mercenary responded, his face deadpan.

"Right, then. At oh-one-hundred hours, I want everybody back down here for cleanup. Anything still living in the joint by then had better be on our side."

He watched the teams led by Thorson and Goldblume as they headed for their separate banks of elevators, leading to the south and east wings of the hotel. His own team would take the north wing in a moment, ride up to the penthouse level and begin their killing at the top.

Abe Bernstein felt that it was going to work this time. Sweet revenge was within his grasp and he could almost taste it now, it was that close. . . .

His troops had reached the elevators, moving like real soldiers as they crossed the wide deserted lobby. Three of Spinoza's watchdogs were lying back behind the registration desk with throats slit, no longer interested in reporting to their boss exactly what was going on beneath his nose.

Spinoza would find out for himself soon enough, and Abe Bernstein was saving that one for himself. He had made certain that his team would be the one to take Spinoza and the others—Johnny Cats, that goddamned Liguori from Chicago—all of them.

A clean frigging sweep. A royal flush, with the Mafia's local royalty flushed right down the goddamned sewer where they all belonged.

"Let's go," he said to no one in particular, already leading out across the lobby, trusting his specials to fall in behind him. He knew that when he turned around they would be there. They were good soldiers and always followed orders.

Abe Bernstein had heard that somewhere, but he could not make the mental linkup and he put the thought away. No time for the abstractions now that they were down to the reality of action.

He was hunting big game now and when the smoke cleared there were going to be some very interesting trophies on his office wall.

LUCY BERNSTEIN POKED HER HEAD out of the office door and took a cautious glance along the corridor in each direction. There was no one in sight and she edged into the open, taking time to close the door behind her, wincing as the locking mechanism clicked audibly into place.

She realized that she was holding her breath and it embarrassed her, but she was still afraid. It was more than an hour since the last paying guests had cleared the Gold Rush, and in that time, instead of digging up the leads she needed for the climax of her exposé, she had been in and out of empty suites and offices, dodging and hiding wherever she could find a door unlocked.

They were not hunting her—not yet—but she felt cut off now, under siege. She had accomplished nothing, losing track of Frank Spinoza and his friend almost at once, and now the only thing that she could think about was getting safely out of there, away from what she sensed was brooding danger.

She had been right, the lady news hawk knew, when she suspected that her grandfather was lying to her.

There had been no labor trouble at the Gold Rush this night, not if all the bellhops and domestic personnel around the place were any indication.

Strange, but now that Lucy stopped to think of it, she had not seen a woman anywhere around the hotel and casino since she'd left the crowded lobby better than an hour ago. It was as if the female staff—the cooks, the maids, whatever—had been cleared away to preserve them from the coming storm.

Now she was all alone inside the cavernous hotel that had so quickly taken on the characteristics of an armed encampment. That was a story in itself, but first she had to be alive to write it—and she feared that if she was discovered, her short career might be abbreviated by a one-way midnight ride into the desert.

Lucy did not plan to end her days as cactus fertilizer, and she moved along the corridor with grim determination, looking for an unobtrusive exit that would get her out of there and on the street again without attracting any unwelcome attention along the way.

She reached the bank of elevators, hesitated with her finger on the button, finally decided against it. If the elevator did not dump her right into the lobby, she would run the risk of being stopped at any one of several floors along the way, or else emerging into hostile hands upon arriving at her destination. No, the elevator simply was not safe enough to suit her needs.

Lucy was turning away from the stainless-steel doors when the approaching sound of voices reached her ears. She hesitated, gauging their direction, bolting as she realized that they were just around the corner from her, closing swiftly.

She retraced her steps and reached the doorway to the office she had just vacated. It was small, belonging to some middle-ranking secretary of Spinoza's from appearances, and it had yielded nothing in her search for information, but right now it was her only sanctuary. Lucy made it to the door with heartbeats left to spare—and found it locked.

She cursed the modern doors that locked themselves each time they closed, and just this once she wished that security had not become such an obsession in the hotel industry.

She turned away, pulse pounding in her ears now that the jumbled voices were almost on top of her. One of them sounded so familiar, somehow, almost—

There was no time to make the connection. She was running blindly, biting off a sob that rose unbidden in her throat. There had to be some service stairs around here someplace, had to be some—

And she found them, almost stumbling as she veered hard left to reach the doorway marked Emergency. If there had ever been one, Lucy thought, this must be it.

She put her weight against the door, expecting hinges stiff with long disuse, and almost fell through as it opened without resistance. She stumbled through, gasping, and just found the strength to close the door behind her.

She was clear.

She took a backward step. . . and bumped against the man who had been standing, watching her.

No stifling the cry this time, as Lucy Bernstein turned and recognized the man she had seen earlier with Frank Spinoza, the same face from her ordeal the night before at Bob Minotte's.

Recognition was mutual and his reaction was as coolly, cruelly practiced as a soldier's own conditioned reflex in the heat of combat.

He took a closer step, the smile etched deep into his face like marks on marble. She saw his fist coming, knew that it was hurtling toward her jaw, and yet she found herself unable to avoid the blow.

Lucy Bernstein's head impacted on the concrete wall behind her and the darkness of the stairwell swallowed her alive.

ABE BERNSTEIN PAUSED outside the doorway of the Gold Rush presidential suite and took the time to brush imaginary lint off of his coat lapels. He wanted to look perfect for the party, give the New York imports something to remember in the final fleeting seconds of their lives.

Finally satisfied, he knocked three times, not loudly, but with firm authority. The sound would carry, and he knew that they were in there, having checked in the several crew chiefs himself.

There would be five of them, not counting their commander who had driven off with Paulie Vaccarelli and the hit team. Five of them with guns and the experience to use them—if they got the chance.

"What is it?"

Curt, discourteous and spoken through the door, as if they had been talking to some newsboy peddling his papers.

"Room service," Bernstein told the faceless voice, struggling to keep contempt and anger from his tone. "Compliments of the management."

As he spoke, he stepped back from the doorway, making room for the three mercenaries to form a semicircle at the entrance of the suite, their silenced Ingram machine pistols already primed and leveled from the waist.

Inside, the nameless crew chief was still fumbling with the lock, then he had it, stepping out to greet them in his shirt-sleeves, one hand resting on a hip beneath his shoulder holster.

And the guy was good, but nowhere close to as good as he thought he was. The little backward step was adequate, the shouted warning excellent, but there was simply no way that his best fast-draw could beat the combined firepower of the three Ingrams. Savage streams of nearly silent fire converged upon him, punching through the fabric of his shirt and letting loose a crimson flood as he was blown away.

The mercenaries entered in a rush, still firing, taking out the other four crew chiefs as they were trying to respond on several seconds' warning. None of them was up to it, although the last one, lurching from the bathroom with an automatic in his hand came closest to achieving some success. He actually got off a shot before two Ingrams sliced and diced him with converging figure eights and draped him back across the leaking water bed.

Bernstein watched from the doorway approvingly, as his commandos brought the bodies all together in the middle of the room and rolled them one by one onto the plastic shower curtain taken from the bathroom. There would be some staining of the carpet even so, and most of it would have to be replaced wherever they encountered opposition, but he wrote it off to the anticipated costs of renovating the hotel.

The Gold Rush was being remodeled, and very soon it would be opening again under the new-old management of its creator. Some new carpeting and wallpaper would help create the aura of a born-again establishment.

"All right, let's go," he snapped, once again consulting the Rolex. "We can't afford to fall behind."

They had three other suites to go before the main event with Frank Spinoza, making sure that he did not have any troops at his beck and call. It was unlikely that the single pistol shot had registered with any of their targets down the hall. But even if they still possessed the slim advantage of surprise, there was no time to waste.

Abe Bernstein meant to have his cleanup finished when the sun came up behind old Sunrise Mountain to the east of town. He meant for this new day to find him in control of the city he had done so much to shape and build.

It was a long time overdue, and he refused to wait an extra moment longer than he absolutely had to.

It was time, and past time, for cleaning house. And now that he had started, nothing in the world would slow him down. Abe Bernstein had a job to do, ordained by fate, and he was working on it with a vengeance.

MACK BOLAN MADE A DRIVE-BY of the Gold Rush, picking out the uniformed security on front and side entrances, noting their numbers and their armament. He sensed that they were bogus, knew it with a certainty when one guard stepped inside and let him glimpse an automatic rifle standing just inside the smoked-glass doors. Still he did not want a confrontation with them there, where innocent civilians might be inadvertently sucked into the cross fire.

He drove around the block and parked his rental in an alleyway behind a liquor store just down the street. Another moment to select and stow his arms, and then he hiked back, taking about thirty seconds to reach the service entrance off Fremont Street.

And they were waiting for him, naturally. He saw them from a half block away, two men in sky-blue uniforms proclaiming them to be Gold Rush security. The mismatched weapons in their holsters told him they were private—still professional, but lacking care for detail and appearances.

As he approached the soldier kept one hand inside the wide slit pocket of his topcoat, wrapped around the Beretta's grip. His finger curled around the trigger in anticipation, and the full weight of the silent weapon in his grasp was reassuring, almost comforting.

A warrior came to trust his weapons, to rely upon them as he might upon a trusted friend. Right now, the lethal 93-R was in good hands—and so was the Executioner.

The guards had noted his approach and they moved

out to head him off. Some brief exchange was whispered softly between them, lost to Bolan's ears. No matter, he did not need to hear them. He was deep inside their minds, anticipating any move they might make.

He knew they would block him, standing shoulder to shoulder across the narrow service entrance when he tried to step around them. On the left, one of them raised a hand, palm outward, with the other resting ominously on his holstered sidearm, like a warning.

"Sorry, sir. We're closed."

"Try back next week," the other one chimed in. "Right now we got some union trouble."

Bolan's smile was icy, but the men were busy looking elsewhere and they never saw it, concentrating as they both were on the hand that poked out of his open top-coat, rising into view and bringing with it silent death.

They saw the weapon simultaneously, each man peeling off in opposite directions with a single practiced motion, going for their weapons, maybe knowing they could never hope to make it.

He took the tall one first, a single measured squeeze dispatching silent death to close the gap between them, a parabellum mangler opening his cheek beneath one eye and boring through to find the brain. The guy kept going through his paces, traveling without a conscious object now, colliding with the wall and then rebounding in a boneless mass across the doorway.

By the time he hit cement, the sentry's partner was a fading memory, wet pieces of himself adhering to the window and the wall behind him where Bolan's single round had exited behind one ear. He sat down hard, no longer reaching for the pistol that was still secure inside his holster.

Bolan checked the alley once again in each direction, taking time to drag the bodies ten feet from the doorway and depositing them together in a waiting dumpster.

They would be there when the trucks from Silver State Disposal came to get them with the other garbage in the morning.

Two down, and how many left to go?

The Executioner had no way of determining the answer in advance, and even if he had been able to predict the odds against him it would not have made a qualitative difference in his actions.

He was here to fight, to spread the cleansing fire among his enemies, and he would carry out that mission whether five guns or five hundred waited for him in the Gold Rush, right.

The Executioner was not a gambler, normally. He much preferred to make his moves on the basis of reconnaissance and hard intelligence, but sometimes there was only time for action.

Like now.

He would be gambling this time, with the highest stakes that any man possessed—his life. But more than that, if he should lose, it would be victory for the cannibals and a defeat for everything that Bolan cherished.

He was up against the house odds, but there were ways around those odds. A skillful player with the guts to stand up and defy the house could sometimes break the bankroll and come out a winner.

Someone with the guts of a warrior. An Executioner, perhaps.

He slipped inside the service entrance, shedding his topcoat to reveal the armament he wore beneath it, moving boldly toward the main casino now.

Mack Bolan's life was riding on the line, and he was playing out the only hand available. It was a death hand, right, and for the moment he was dealing.

22

Spinoza faced the woman across his desk, reading the fear in her eyes and knowing he could use that fear against her, given time. She would say anything, do anything he asked her to when he was finished with her.

Given time.

But time was one commodity that he was running short of, and the others with him in the room—Liguori, Johnny Cats, and Tommy Dioguardi, from Minotte's family—were taking every opportunity to let him know of their impatience.

They were chafing at the bit, unsettled by the news from Kuwahara's. Paulie and the gunners from New York had run into a storm out there, and from all reports the few of them who walked away from it were looking at six-figure bail, for openers. It would take time to get them out—the ones who were not hospitalized already—and meantime the chieftains who were gathered at the Gold Rush had begun to feel exposed, unprotected.

Spinoza was not worried. There were still some forty guns at the hotel, and even if that bastard Kuwahara was alive, he would be tied up with the cops until they sorted out the shooting down in Paradise. *If* he was still alive, Spinoza meant to find it out and have a hot reception waiting for him when he made his bail, damn right. A welcome-home party that the little Nip would long remember.

As for the woman. . . .

It was disturbing, Dioguardi's story of her showing up at Bob Minotte's just before the raid that took the Southern capo's life. She did not have the lethal look about her, but Spinoza had learned never to take anything for granted when it came to life and death. He put no faith at all in blind coincidence, and that meant she had a reason for her presence at Minotte's, and now here, in the Gold Rush.

Whatever that purpose might be, he meant to find it out within the hour.

By any means necessary.

"All right, let's try it one more time," he said. "I want your name, the reason that you're here...and after this is settled, we can all relax. You can go home."

"Like hell—" Liguori started to intrude, but Frank Spinoza raised a hand and cut him off.

"Excuse my friends," he said, forcing a smile. "They're just a bit excited—and they don't take kindly to trespassers, eavesdroppers...that kind of thing."

The woman sat mute, just staring back at him, and underneath the fear, there was something else—a kind of grim determination, maybe, that told Spinoza to expect resistance.

Fine.

He had encountered stubborn types before, and where persuasion failed, the application of strategic force was often more effective.

Spinoza reached inside his top desk drawer, drew out the Browning automatic and set it on the desk between them with its muzzle pointed in the woman's direction.

"Now. I understand you're scared," he told her. "And you've got good reason. If I don't get answers from you pretty quick...well, I can't be responsible for what might happen to you."

"I've got nothing to say," she informed him, her voice small and quaking. "You're holding me against my will. That's kidnapping. I'll stack that against a trespass charge any day, so go ahead and call the police.''

''When I'm ready.'' Spinoza felt his smile going, but could not retrieve it in time. ''First thing, I'm going to have those answers.''

Silence once again and another toss of the head that set her hair in dancing motion all around her face.

''Goddamn it, Frank—''

''Shut up, Larry. Leave this to me.''

And he could feel the others staring at him in amazement, wondering where he found the guts to talk that way to other capos, but Spinoza was no longer worried about their reactions. He raised the pistol, circling the desk to stand before the woman, and bent down, his face mere inches from her own.

''I'll ask you one more time,'' he said, and there was no mistaking the menace in his tone.

''Go to hell.''

He hit her with his open palm, the shock of it exploding up his arm with stunning force. Her head rocked back, blood spurting from her nose, and when she opened her eyes again she had the dazed expression of a shell-shock victim. Frank Spinoza gave her time to clear her head before he stuck the pistol in her face and cocked the hammer.

''One *last* time,'' he told her now. ''I want some answers and you'd better be convincing.''

He was giddy with the power of the moment, knowing that he could do anything he wanted to with this one. He could blow her head off, throw her on the desk and take her then and there with all the others watching... anything.

The others....

When he finished with the woman, he had plans for them as well. There would be rounds enough inside the

Browning's magazine for everyone. A clean sweep, sure, and too long overdue.

The capo of Las Vegas smiled, a reptile's grimace, full of hunger unfulfilled.

BOLAN CLEARED THE SERVICE AREA and made his way in the direction of the large casino proper, moving cautiously, scanning the corridors to either side of him. He held the Mini-Uzi ready, waiting to respond to any hostile challenge, knowing that the savages were all around him now. The problem would be finding them, rooting them out and destroying them without walking into an ambush.

And he found them thirty feet along the corridor as he was passing by an office doorway with the legend Private painted on it. As he passed the door it swung open and a startled face confronted him, mouth working silently for several seconds as the brain attempted to translate its silent warning into sound.

The guy recovered instantly at sight of Bolan's rising Uzi. He leaped backward, slamming the door behind him and fumbling with the locking mechanism. And he had his voice back now, alerting anyone in earshot to the danger of an armed intruder in their midst.

Bolan stitched a burst across the flimsy door, then hit it with a flying kick that tore the lock apart, following through into a diving shoulder roll. He caught a glimpse of hardman number one slumped back against a filing cabinet, clutching at the bloody ruin of his punctured abdomen. Others were unloading on him now with handguns, and he let the dying take care of themselves.

Two of them were crouched behind a massive metal desk, taking turns at popping up to fire in his direction. A third was holed up in a tiny back room that appeared to serve as combination lounge and storeroom. Bolan pinned the two desk gunners down with probing fire and scuttled backward to the cover of another unattended desk that faced their sanctuary from across the room.

It was a weak position, right, with space beneath the desk for ricochets to find him if they started thinking straight instead of firing out of reflex. Worse, they had the chance to pin him down until sufficient reinforcements could arrive to rush him.

The Executioner would have to move swiftly if he meant to stay alive. Another moment might be all the time he had.

Bolan sprang a frag grenade from his combat harness, pulled the pin and let it fly, already counting down. The pitch was perfect, even under fire, deflecting off metal filing cabinets to drop down behind the desk, between the hostile gunners in their little foxhole.

"What the. . .!"

And that was all before the blast eclipsed their screaming voices, toppling the desk and spreading both of them across the walls like lumpy red wallpaper. A piece of shrapnel clipped the wounded gunner where he stood transfixed for a moment. Then he slid into the graceless sprawl of death.

Three down and number four was screaming in his little pantry hideaway, half-blinded by the smoke and deafened by the harsh concussion of the blast. He lost it, lurching up and out of cover, firing blindly as he cleared the narrow doorway with no more idea of where his target was than if he had been shooting at the moon.

Bolan tracked him through the doorway, stroking off a three-round burst that picked the gunner off his feet and twisted him around, a human corkscrew, airborne, sprawling back across the smoking desk. Before the body finished twitching, the Executioner was up and out of there, already moving back along the corridor to the casino, searching for the action.

And it was just ahead of him, the Executioner could

hear it now, the jangle of the play replaced now by the pop and crackle of small-arms fire.

Someone had engaged the enemy in there, and they were not firing at him—at least not yet.

Mack Bolan dropped the Uzi's magazine and snapped a fresh one into place, no longer walking now, but jogging toward the sounds of battle. They had started the bloodfeast without him but the Executioner was coming. Better late than never, right.

He was one of the invited guests whether the hosts were currently aware of it or not.

The Executioner had been invited by the Universe.

ABE BERNSTEIN REACHED INSIDE HIS JACKET, pulling out the short slim automatic pistol from his waistband. He took a moment, checking out the action, waiting while old Harry Thorson slid a new clip into the receiver of his Army-model .45.

They had regrouped for the assault on Frank Spinoza's penthouse, Bernstein refusing to take any chances when they had come so far and dared so much to make it work. They would be done with it tonight or none of them could count on a tomorrow—in Las Vegas or anywhere.

If Frank Spinoza or another of the capos in there managed to escape with news of what Abe Bernstein had accomplished at the Gold Rush, they could write it off as a total loss.

"All set?"

He glanced around and noticed that Jack Goldblume held his pistol pointed to the floor as if he was afraid it might go off and hurt someone. Old Jack was looking green around the gills, as if the sights that he had witnessed there that evening had been almost more than he could stomach.

Almost, but not entirely. He was with them still, and

Bernstein meant to make sure that he stayed there—at least until they finished with Spinoza and the others. He still needed the *Beacon*, a sympathetic press, to help cover their tracks when they were finished. Later, when the smoke had cleared and the dust of battle settled. . . .

Well, Jack Goldblume was looking more expendable by the moment.

Abe's prey was in there, waiting for him now. Not taking any chances, he had risked a phone call from the last suite they had visited, putting on his best solicitous flunky's voice and asking Frank if there was anything that he could do for any of them. Coffee? Liquor? Anything at all?

Spinoza had cut him off, but not before Abe had heard the other voices in the background, jabbering excitedly together, arguing in angry tones.

Liguori.

Catalanotte.

Dioguardi.

A clean sweep, bet your ass.

"Let's go."

He nodded to the pair of mercenaries waiting by the doorway to the penthouse, and they stepped in front of it, their silenced Ingrams leveled from the waist. One of them hit the locking mechanism with a short precision burst and they followed through, the others crowding in behind them, Bernstein jockeying into a firing-line position, letting Thorson and Jack Goldblume ride his coattails.

And his men were under orders not to fire until he gave the order. One last precaution, time to let him verify the targets before the heads began to roll.

He stood there gaping in amazement and shock at the tableau laid out before his eyes. At first the visual impulse made no sense, and then he realized that it was no illusion.

Bernstein saw the woman seated in the chair with her hands bound behind her. He made the recognition through a veil of caking blood that ran down from her nose, her lips, a cut above one eye.

Spinoza stood above her, one fist poised to strike again. Behind him the other capos ranged around the desk, their enjoyment of the sport interrupted by the intrusion.

Something cold and deadly rose in Bernstein's throat and he raised the pistol, aiming it at Frank Spinoza's chest before the thought could translate into conscious images.

"You bastard!"

"Wait a minute, Abe—"

And there was something in Spinoza's hand, a pistol, Bernstein saw, but he ignored it. Squeezing off a round, he watched the slug drill through Spinoza's throat, releasing bloody plumes that splattered down his shirt front, soaking through.

Another round, and one of Frank Spinoza's eyes exploded from its socket, hurtling across the room. The man was dead now but he would not fall. Bernstein kept on firing, emptying his magazine into the standing corpse, until the point-blank impact threw him backward, stretched him out across the cluttered desk.

The other capos were reacting, alternately diving for some cover they could never hope to reach, or grasping after weapons of their own. The mercenaries opened fire, and Abe could hear the roar of Harry Thorson's .45 as he joined in. But Abe was heedless of the cross fire now, already kneeling down at Lucy's side and slicing at her bonds with a penknife he carried.

Of the mafiosi, only Johnny Cats had time to reach his weapon and employ it, squeezing off three rounds before converging streams of fire crucified him to the wall. The others died in varied attitudes of flight, devoid of honor, courage—everything but fear.

Abe Bernstein felt the tears as he released his granddaughter from her confinement in the straight-backed
chair. His taste of victory had turned to something sour
in his throat, threatening to gag him as he knelt there
looking at her swollen bloodied face.

He told her he was sorry, begged her to forgive him,
but she did not seem to hear. At last he motioned for a
couple of his soldiers to assist him, and he lifted her out
of the chair, got her onto her feet and held her there until she found the strength to stand.

"Let's get you home," he said, as if a change of scene
would make things right again, erase the sights and
memories of what had happened here this night.

"Let's get you home," he said again, and knew she
was not hearing him.

Abe Bernstein turned back toward the door, one arm
around his grandchild's shoulders. He saw Jack Goldblume stretched out on the carpet, Harry Thorson bending over him and feeling for a pulse against his throat.
The newsman's jacket, shirt and all were soaking crimson where the rounds from Johnny Cats's last burst had
caught him, and Abe knew that it was hopeless long
before the cowboy straightened up and shook his head.

"No good, Abe."

"Okay, we'll take him with the others. Hurry."

And they were not finished yet, he knew. There were
still stragglers to be dealt with in the Gold Rush, and
disposal teams to organize. Transporting all the bodies
would be no small undertaking in itself, and Bernstein
wondered where he might locate a garbage truck at this
hour of the night.

No matter. First, he had to care for Lucy, make her
understand that what had happened was an accident, a
side effect of what he had achieved for all of them this
night.

For all of Vegas.

It would take time, he knew, but she would understand once he explained it to her from the start. If he could take her back to the beginning, when the town was young and so was he, before the leeches came to fasten on him, draining off his life's blood.

They reached the escalator and Abe Bernstein forced himself to concentrate on here and now. Before he could tell Lucy anything, they had to get out of the hotel in one piece. And from the sounds downstairs, that might be difficult.

The old catch phrase came back to him—something they used to say all the time during the war. What was it, now?

"The difficult we do at once. The impossible takes a little longer."

Well, he had accomplished the impossible already here tonight. The difficult would prove no match for him, with victory already within his grasp.

Abe Bernstein checked the little automatic's load and slipped it back inside the waistband of his slacks as he followed his mercenaries onto the moving staircase. He could smell the battle now below them, as well as hear it echoing around the vast casino. Lucy vanished from his thoughts immediately, and the hunter reemerged, triumphant.

23

Bolan found the main casino of the Gold Rush shrouded in a pall of drifting battle smoke when he emerged out of the concourse into open view. The center of the room, along the line of vacant roulette tables, had become a lethal no-man's land. Fire teams were off to either side, intent on gaining ground and laying down a steady fusillade that ricocheted from slot machines and ceiling fixtures, gouging ragged chunks of plaster from the walls.

It seemed as if the hotel staff had risen up in arms against the tenants, with a line of bellhops and blue-uniformed security staked out on Bolan's left, the business suits and shirt-sleeves of the Mafia gunners on his right. And Bolan did not need a cast of characters to know that he was witnessing an overthrow of Frank Spinoza's hoodlum empire.

To be replaced by what? Abe Bernstein and his good-old boys? A second-generation syndicate that Bernstein might have put together, waiting in the wings?

Bolan had no time for thinking futures. There was ample trouble in his present to keep him occupied. And if he played his cards right it would matter little what the mafiosi or their opposition might be planning.

The Executioner announced his entry to the battle with a pair of frag grenades among the hostile soldiers. He was already moving when the two eggs detonated into smoky thunder, less than a second apart, seeking cover from the answering fire that could not be far behind. They were still screaming out there, as he reached a bank of slots and hunkered down behind the one-armed bandits, waiting for the storm to break around him.

Downrange a Mafia gunner poked his head around the line of slots, angling for a shot when Bolan took his face off with a short burst from the Uzi. The guy's pistol went off aimlessly as he impacted with the carpet, one stray round careening off polished chrome above Bolan's head.

The warrior moved, knowing that the surest way to die in combat was to make yourself a stationary target. He was virtually surrounded now, but neither side could be sure who he was or what his unexpected entry to the three-ring charnel circus might portend for their side. By the time they had an answer, Bolan planned to be on top of things, dealing from strength and calling the tune in their impromptu dance of death.

He covered for himself with automatic fire and kept on moving, never pausing long enough for hostile guns to find him. More than one was silenced by the probing bursts from Bolan's stuttergun, and now the fire from one side to another had begun to falter, gunners hesitating as they tried a rapid battlefield assessment of the latest threat.

Bolan could not give them time to think. He plucked another frag can from his belt and yanked the pin, counting down the seconds to doomsday as he chose a target randomly and let the bomb fly. Across the narrow no-man's land, a crap table took flight, all four legs off the ground and levitating on a ball of flame before it settled back to earth in smoking ruins. In the wake of the explosion, Bolan heard the death screams mingling with the clash of small-arms fire and someone shouting for instructions from his crew chief.

He emptied the Uzi in one searing burst, saw two of

the blue-uniformed security guards topple underneath the driving rain of parabellum hornets. Swiftly he reloaded, moving out of there in search of other sanctuary before the hostiles could react.

He reached a blackjack table, overturned already in the heat of battle. He hurdled it, touching down behind the barricade in combat readiness. The warrior was prepared for anything—except, perhaps, to face the mafioso who already occupied that makeshift foxhole, gaping at him now from no more than three feet away, the pistol he extended in his right hand touching-close.

No time to think, and Bolan chopped at the extended wrist with his free hand, swinging the Uzi around like a club toward the other man's face, simultaneously squeezing off a ragged burst at skin-touch range. The chopper's stubby muzzle struck the gunner's skull...and then that skull was vaporized, with scalp and brain and all of it departing in a pink mist.

Bolan felt the man's life blood now as it trickled down his cheeks, befouled his hair and clothing. But the Executioner held the trigger down until the clip had spent its load and he was staring at the headless body of a onetime enemy stretched out on the blood-soaked carpet.

Bolan wiped the mess off his face as he rose to a crouch. He was reaching for another magazine to feed the starving Uzi when he saw the little party coming down the escalator, right into the middle of the flagging action. More security, their sky-blues stained from battle on the upper floors, and there behind them, someone else.

The woman, right.

He knew the old man standing on her right and half-supporting her would be Abe Bernstein. The old man was in charge of what had happened here tonight—or rather, had been, until fate had found a wild card named Mack Bolan in the deck.

No time now for the Uzi, as the mercenaries on the

escalator opened fire upon their mafiosi targets. They were swift, professional and deadly with those silenced Ingrams, raking back and forth and blowing holes along the hostile ranks before their presence registered on shell-shocked minds. Another moment. . .less, and they could turn the tide to victory for their side.

Bolan ripped the AutoMag out of its military leather, thumbing back the hammer as he sighted quickly down the muzzle, making target acquisition at a range of something under forty yards. Lucy Bernstein was in danger, but he could not afford to let her clear the danger zone.

There were no havens here tonight as long as one last cannibal remained alive. The warrior's mission was to kill them all. And failing that, to wound them savagely, to drive them undercover, bloodied, hurting, thinking twice before they dared to show their jackal faces in the sunlight one more time.

The Executioner was living out his mission, right, performing to the utmost of his duty. He would spare the woman if he could, but in the last analysis she had to take her chances with the rest of them.

There were no house odds any more around the Gold Rush. Every rule was canceled now, with wild cards in the game, and it was down to one last hand—winner take all.

Mack Bolan braced the mighty AutoMag in both hands and placed his bet.

THE MAIN CASINO FLOOR was in a bloody shambles, and Abe Bernstein shook his head, unable to believe his eyes. A simple mopping-up had rapidly degenerated into chaos, and he sensed that they could lose it unless they moved decisively to stem the running tide.

The Mafia troops were up against the southern bank of slots, pinned and fighting tenaciously for their lives. They might break out of their position, rush the exits, make it to the street outside, and—

No! It was imperative that all of them be killed. Bernstein barked an order to the mercenaries who surrounded him. At once they formed a spearhead, opened fire upon the Mafia entrenchments, scoring hits immediately with their cold precision fire.

They could still save it, with swift, audacious action, and Abe Bernstein felt another rush, the hot adrenaline now pumping through his ancient veins and giving him his second wind. He brushed past Lucy, plucking at the pistol in his waistband, anxious to be in the finish line, the climax of his dreams.

He saw the man in black peripherally, a rising shadow with a massive silver cannon in his fist. Bernstein flinched away from that impending danger, survivor's instinct taking over like the old days, conscious thought replaced by reflex action.

Bernstein heard the shot—that's good; you never hear the one that kills you—and he felt the hot wind as the Magnum round passed by him, missing by a hair's breadth, ripping into Harry Thorson's ample belly.

Harry toppled forward, gasping, clutching both hands to his wounded abdomen and making no attempt to catch himself before he fell. He hit the mercenaries down in front of him, a massive flying tackle from behind, and then all four of them were rolling in a human knot of tangled arms and legs along the humming risers of the escalator, tumbling down twenty feet toward the landing.

Below him, Bernstein heard the cannon roar again, and he was moving, but too slowly this time. Something struck his shoulder with sledgehammer force, knocking him completely off his feet. He was conscious of the stairsteps rushing up to meet him, metal slicing deep into his cheek. Then his face collided with the heel of Harry's boot at the bottom of the moving staircase, grounded, with the others coming down on top of him.

He searched about him for the pistol, knew that it was gone, and settled for the Army .45 that Harry had somehow kept hold of when he died. For a fleeting instant Lucy crossed his mind, but now survival was the only thought as he gripped the captured pistol, struggling to his feet among the twisted, tangled bodies, fighting to maintain his balance.

The small-arms fire had momentarily trailed away to nothing on his flanks, and he was conscious only of the big man crouching behind the cover of a blackjack table. This one, this *meshugeneh* commando, was all his.

This one who dared to challenge Abe Bernstein when he was so close to living out his dream.

The old man thumbed the safety off of Harry's .45 and staggered across the prostrate body of his friend, unconscious of the pounding in his chest, the throbbing of his own pulse in his ears. He had a job to finish and it lay ahead of him.

He raised the pistol, sighted quickly down the barrel and squeezed the trigger.

BOLAN SAW THE OLD MAN coming for him, and he waited, knowing he could end it, here and now, with only minor mopping-up left over for Sam Reese and Homicide. He counted down the numbers, letting Bernstein find his weapon, lift it, get the feel of iron that could not save him now.

His first shot was a good foot off, the second closer, but not much. Mack Bolan sighed into the squeeze and rode the Magnum's recoil, keeping both eyes open to assess the shot, make sure there would be no need for a second.

Downrange, old Abe Bernstein took 240 grains of sudden revelation in the chest and vaulted backward, stretching out across the jumbled bodies of the aging cowboy and the shaken mercenaries. Some of them were stirring now, recovering from their spill. Bolan put them back to sleep forever, emptying the autoloader into anything and everything that moved around the escalator.

Everything except the woman.

She was cringing down to one side of the carnage, eyes closed, hands pressed tight across her ears, and Bolan's fire was never closer to her than a yard away.

She did not see the old man die, or watch the others twitching, writhing with the impact of his Magnum rounds. No part of her was watching when the others cut and run, the few live stragglers making for the exits now, their guns and grudge forgotten as they tried to beat the clock and win a race with Death itself.

Mack Bolan let them go, no longer interested in the privates now that generals had been dealt with. They might regroup or simply scatter to the winds, but either way, the ones who left the Gold Rush running had been taught a lesson. They had seen death and knew that it could cut both ways.

Lucy flinched when Bolan touched her shoulder, lurched away from him a moment prior to making recognition. When she saw his bloodstained face, the tears came, and she rushed to meet him, arms locked tight around his neck, her body molded tight against his own in something very much like desperation.

"Take me out of here," she whispered fiercely. "Please take me out of here."

He took her out of there, back along the darkened alley to his waiting rental car, the rising song of sirens now replacing ghostly echoes of the gunfire in his ears. Captain Reese, right, bringing in the cavalry to save the day. A trifle late, but then again the day might be worth saving, after all.

EPILOGUE

4-057894S345 3/9/85 ICS IPMRNCZ CSP LSAB
213684534 MGM TDRN LAS VEGAS NV 44 3-9 0521A
EST
JOHNNY B GRAY
1135 ACROPOLIS
SAN DIEGO CA
THE DESERT IS ABOUT TO BLOOM AGAIN STOP
EAST WINDS WERE OVERRATED AND THE
STORM IS PAST FOR NOW STOP HOPE ALL IS
WELL AT STRONGBASE, AND THAT WE MAY BE
TOGETHER SOON STOP PLEASE KEEP ADVISED
ON U.S. SITUATION WHILE I AM OVERSEAS
STOP LOOKING FORWARD TO SOME WELCOME
R&R AT YOUR LOCATION, SOONEST STOP LIVE
LARGE STOP
ALL LOVE,
M

MORE ADVENTURE NEXT MONTH WITH

MACK BOLAN

#76 Teheran Wipeout

A time bomb is ticking in Iran

Ayatollah Khomeini, a power-mad tyrant, is using religion to mesmerize his people and enforce his crazed will.

Thousands of Iranians are butchered in acts that are pitching the country into a relentless downward spiral toward the Dark Ages.

Combat specialist Mack Bolan answers a call from rebel forces to help save a once-great nation from certain doom.

Available soon wherever paperbacks are sold.

Excerpts from
THE PENDLETON TAPES

No. 2 in an occasional series

From *"Denver at Noon"*

Renée Hambley reporting on KMGH-TV, Denver, Colorado.

Hambley: Don Pendleton holds the distinction of creating a new genre of fiction by writing an action-adventure series called The Executioner. We have asked Mr. Pendleton to be with us, and today he is our guest. Let's talk about Mack Bolan—I picture him as very handsome.

Pendleton: All right!

Hambley: Why do you think he is so popular?

Pendleton: Because he's the personification of what most people like in a man, whether it be a woman or a man who is reading the book. I have tried to construct this character, Bolan, to epitomize the responsible, compassionate human beings that are the most admirable in our society. Soldiers, for example.

Hambley: That's a paradox, isn't it? That a soldier can have compassion?

Pendleton: Yes, it is paradoxical. Soldiers are people who are willing to compromise their own private sense of human ethics in order to say, "I will kill. I will kill to uphold the forward movement of mankind."

Hambley: How would you describe Mack Bolan to someone who had never read your books before?

Pendleton: First off, he is a man with whom you would feel comfortable in your own home. He's a warm, compassionate man, and it is because of his compassion and his humanity that he's doing the things he's doing. He is always a very violent figure, there's no doubt about that, but Bolan sees the human race as a family, as his family, and he's deeply concerned about what's happening to them.

Hambley: I realize now that you have a cult following. One of our station personnel was down at the bookstore while you were doing a signing, and he told the people there that he'd never heard of you. Well, they all said, what, are you crazy? Don Pendleton—*everyone* knows him! What do you think is the reason for this wide acclaim?

Pendleton: If there is any acclaim at all, it's because I tell the truth. There are a lot of rip-offs out there, but as soon as you read the opening chapters of an Executioner book, right away you know that it's the real thing. I tell the reader that there are two kinds of violence. There is the destructive violence that tears down the human estate, and there is the necessary counterviolence needed to maintain the civilized world and a semblance of order. I think that is a realistic, truthful assessment of the way things have to be.

Hambley: So will violence always be with us?

Pendleton: Look, one psycho with a switch-blade knife could come in here and dominate, take this television station over, unless there were one person in here willing to counter that violence with some of his own. We simply cannot give in to the savages.

Hambley: Then will there always be savages?

Pendleton: When I say "savages," I don't mean primitive people. I mean those people who will not conform to the civilized ideal. We have savages in business suits sitting in corporate offices in this country—many of the Bolan books depict such men. Savages will proliferate in all areas of society as long as there is no one to stand up against them.

Hambley: Tell us how you do your research.

Pendleton: I go to the place where the book is going to be set, and I set the book according to what's happening in the world. But the world has become so incredible, you know, that trying to work a year ahead of publication date and still be current is very difficult. The writer must keep the world believable, with information that the reader can readily assimilate, at the same time as the world itself becomes increasingly indescribable. It's the writer's job to make his fiction more real than the real world, and that's tough today. Even our wildest plots tend to turn up in the headlines, in news stories that are far wilder than what our readers would be prepared to accept in the books. The terrorist madness of the Libyan regime, and the 1984 Japanese plot to poison supermarket food, are two cases in point. Long before those events we invented stories that would reflect the possibility of such situations occurring in the modern world, but they pale compared with the way the real events actually went down. Many of our facts, however, were almost clairvoyant in their accuracy.

Hambley: Accuracy's a big thing with you and your staff, isn't it?

Pendleton: Yeah, it has to be. I don't like to put a strange weapon in Bolan's hands. I don't like to put him on unfamiliar ground. I really do have to go and research the locales beforehand. And I've used all the weapons that Bolan has, but I'm not quite the marksman he is.

Hambley: How did you research the original Mafia stories? Was that more difficult?

Pendleton: I would pick a city where things were happening and go and talk to law-enforcement people, people in the press who worked the police beats, try to get a meeting with someone in the Mob, or if that couldn't be arranged, with someone very close.

Hambley: And you'd get the meeting?

Pendleton: Oh, yes. I was speaking with Sam Giancana only three weeks before he was gunned down in the elevator of a hotel in Chicago. And just a short while later, I was in San Diego on a book promotion and Frank Bompensiero, the don of San Diego, was killed in just about the same fashion. I began to worry if I was carrying a jinx around with me!

Hambley: I was just going to say. . . because I guess the Mob gives a lot of thought to you.

Pendleton: Not really. A lot of the people in the Mob are fans, strangely enough. They read the books and like them. Of course, everybody likes stories about the Mafia. I was talking to a kid who'd seen the first *Godfather* movie seventeen times, but the movie had only been out for seventeen days, so he must have gone back every day. Just goes to show.

Hambley: Before our time's up, can we talk briefly about the movie that's coming out? Burt Reynolds is going to produce it?

Pendleton: That's right, and Sylvester Stallone will write, direct and star in the picture—maybe a series of pictures. Burt has been a fan for a long time, and finally he came to see me and asked if we could get something going. He's such a nice man. I'm really glad that he and Sly are the ones that will be bringing the books to the screen. I'm so excited about that.

Hambley: I should think so. Don, will you bring Burt with you the next time you come?

Pendleton: I'll have him right here in my back pocket!

Hambley: You've got a deal. Thank you for speaking with us, Don Pendleton, and we wish you luck with your books.

Pendleton: Thank you, Renée, thank you so much.

GET THE
NEW WAR BOOK
AND MACK BOLAN
BUMPER STICKER <u>FREE!</u>
Mail this coupon today!

Mack Bolan is a Winner!

Readers everywhere applaud his success.

"You deserve some kind of reward for delivering such reading pleasure to millions of people throughout the world."

M.L.,* Chicago, Illinois

"Bolan isn't a killer—he is a positive force fighting the degeneration of man. He is also awesomely entertaining, as fine a literary hero as any."

S.S., Augsburg, Germany

"I want to congratulate you on your decision to put our Sergeant into the fight against terrorism. With the world situation today, it will endear many more people to this man of courage."

B.C., New York, New York

"I am in the army, and I would be proud to serve with Mack Bolan and cover his back down the first mile, and second, and third if he said it was needed."

P.E.D., APO, New York

"I think my Executioner collection is the finest thing I own, or probably ever will own."

R.C., Gainesville, Florida

*Names available on request.